THE GIRL FROM NOWHERE

GIRL FROM NOWHERE

Rae Foley

Chivers Press • Thorndike Press
Bath, Avon, England   Thorndike, Maine USA

AM GH ZE NG MA ID PU

This Large Print edition is published by Chivers Press, England
and by Thorndike Press, USA.

Published in 1995 in the U.K. by arrangement with the Golden West
Literary Agency.

Published in 1995 in the U.S. by arrangement with the Golden West
Literary Agency.

U.K. Hardcover ISBN 0–7451–2659–6 (Chivers Large Print)
U.S. Softcover   ISBN 0–7862–0191–6 (General Series Edition)

The text of this Large Print edition is unabridged.
Other aspects of the book may vary from the original edition.

Set in 16 pt. New Times Roman.

Printed in Great Britain on acid-free paper.

British Library Cataloguing in Publication Data available

Library of Congress Cataloging-in-Publication Data

Foley, Rae, 1900–
   Girl from nowhere / Rae Foley.
     p. cm.
   ISBN 0–7862–0191–6 (alk. paper : lg. print)
   1. Large type books. I. Title.
[PS3511.O186G57 1995]
813'.54—dc20
                                        94–1083

For Dorothy Abel

CHAPTER ONE

When the waiter had pulled out the table, the girl and her companion slid onto the curved red-leather bench. As he pushed the table back the waiter's mouth tightened with disapproval. He was a family man himself. What were the girl's people thinking of? She was too young to be dining alone with a fellow of this sort. Cute as a button, too, in that white evening gown, as though she had dressed up for the first time in her life. The gown, like her escort, was too old for her, but it set off the golden tan of her arms and shoulders.

The waiter took their orders, managing swift, discreet glances at them while they consulted the menu. The girl had a triangular face and an appealing way with her. The man, seedy and down at heel, wasn't her class at all. She had to explain how to order in a first-rate place like this and her unpleasant companion did not like having his ignorance shown up. There was a flush on the unnatural pallor of his face whenever he looked at her. From her laughing reassurance the girl made it plain that she was paying for the meal. And she was not the kind who had to pay for her company either. Not with her looks.

Fooled by a hard-luck story, the waiter decided sagely. Letting this character take advantage of the kindness of her heart. And the kid meant well. Too young to know men.

Her companion looked about twenty-eight; less, perhaps; but there was no youth in him, no zest, no eagerness. When the girl spoke, a kind of spasm crossed his drawn young-old face, a flickering of hope that flared up and died down and never quite went out, as though it were the last spark of life in him, unwilling to be extinguished. The menu shook in his hands. When he looked up unexpectedly, as though hoping to trap the waiter off guard and discover whether he was being watched, the pupils of his eyes were visibly contracted to mere pinpoints. There ought to be a law, the waiter thought in righteous indignation.

'Two Martinis,' he told the bartender, 'and make one of them weak. That girl's too young to be drinking.'

The bartender followed his eyes. 'Quite a babe,' he remarked. The bartender was not a family man. He followed the cunning lines of the white dress with pleasure. The girl was put together according to Hollywood specifications. 'That's the kind of dress I like,' he said. 'No guess work about it.'

A few moments later the waiter returned to the bar and slammed down a Martini glass. 'She thinks you forgot the gin.'

The bartender's job had taught him to keep his mouth shut so he mixed another cocktail and refrained from making any comment.

2

When the waiter brought the Martini the second time the girl sipped it and nodded. 'That's more like it.'

Her escort raised his glass. 'Well, Tony, here's to old times.'

'It's marvelous, seeing you again, Alvin,' she said, her eyes wide and candid. They moved on to the next table where a man was openly staring at her, unmindful of the annoyance of the two women with him.

'I hope you mean that,' Alvin said so timidly that the girl struggled to conceal her irritation. 'You didn't seem glad when I met you on the street this afternoon.' He dropped his hands under the table and pulled down his sleeves to cover the frayed cuffs of his shirt.

'Darling, I was tired and hot and thinking about something else. And so surprised. I never dreamed you would turn up in New York after all this time.'

'I told you it would be a year. It's only taken me ten months,' he reminded her. 'Not so bad, considering I didn't have a job.'

'How did you get here?' she asked without curiosity.

'Skip it.'

She was more alert now. 'Come on,' she said laughing, 'tell me about it.'

'I stole a car,' he admitted. 'I left it in Newark and came over on the Tubes. To look for you. Why didn't you write, Tony? I didn't have any address. And then, after three days, to run spang into you on Fifth Avenue!' He pushed away a bowl of flowers. 'If you hadn't been in such a hurry when we met, I'd never have let you sell me on a place like this.'

She glanced around in apparent surprise. 'What's the matter with it?'

'Too rich for my blood.'

'But, darling, I told you I was paying.'

He flushed again. 'Yes, you made that clear.'

She stole a glance at his face. 'I'm sorry,' she said softly. 'We're such old friends I never thought you'd mind.'

'Didn't you?'

Her face hardened. 'If you are going to be disagreeable, Alvin—'

The sneer faded from his face. 'Don't be mad at me,' he said anxiously. 'Please, Tony! I just thought it would be different—that we'd go up to your place, wherever you're staying—like we used to—and talk. Oh, Tony, I'd forgotten how you look—how—' He ran his finger under his collar. 'I got to thinking there might be some other man and I nearly went mad.'

She moved one round shoulder in a gesture of contempt and then laid her hand over his. 'The budget runs to another drink before dinner,' she informed him so sweetly that it checked his resentment at her choice of phrase.

He looked down at the soft hand, at the platinum band and the big solitaire. His face twitched with a kind of spasm.

'You're married!' He took the cocktail at a

4

gulp. 'How long ago did that happen?'

Her soft fingers moved in a futile gesture to conceal the rings. She shrugged her shoulders; she could handle him.

'Six months.'

He crumbled a roll in his fingers. There was no color in his face now, no color in his lips. 'You'd been here only four months.' He tried to laugh. 'What took you so long?'

'We had to wait for his wife to get a divorce.'

'You're a cool one, Tony. By the lord Harry, you are.' There was a kind of wonder in his voice.

'It was love at first sight,' she said demurely.

'Save that for someone else. You fell in love with those emeralds.'

Her fingers stroked the glittering necklace. 'You're wrong, Alvin. This is the first time I've ever worn it.' There was an aggrieved droop to her mouth. Then, with one of her chameleon changes, it became pathetic. 'Why did you want to see me if you dislike me so much?'

Water splashed over the edge of the tumbler and he steadied it with his other hand. 'You mustn't talk like that. I'm crazy about you. And how you know it!'

'I do know it,' she said. 'Let's not quarrel, Alvin, when we mean so much to each other.'

For a moment his pain-filled eyes saw her clearly. 'You never gave a damn for anyone in your life.'

At his tone she felt a little shiver of

5

excitement, aware of danger. 'You know better than that.' She laughed as his tired, tormented face flushed again.

'Then why couldn't you wait for me?'

The triangular eyes rested on the worn sleeves of his coat. 'I didn't want to be a burden to you.'

He hadn't missed the look. 'Sure, I'm short of cash. But selling out to an old gent—a girl like you—'

'Carey is thirty-five and very good looking.'

'Yeah?' Alvin was thoughtful. 'And he doesn't mind you going out with another man?'

'He's out himself. Business with a client.' She giggled.

'What's so funny about that?'

'Maybe I'll tell you some time.'

'You don't think I'd make you any trouble, honey?'

'Not you,' she said oddly.

'No risk of running into him, is there?' He sat erect and she noticed the shoulder blades sharp under the shabby coat.

'Afraid?'

'Not at all. I'd like to see what he's got besides emerald necklaces.'

That remark seemed to amuse Tony and Alvin began to watch her unobtrusively.

'You won't see Carey here,' she told him. 'He doesn't patronize obscure restaurants even where the food is famous. He's a public relations man and he has to go places where he can be seen and where he can point out celebrities to his clients. The Stork and 21—you know.'

'Like hell I do. Flying high, aren't you?'

'Don't be cross, angel. I can't bear it. You're coming home with me after dinner. I want you to see our place.'

*   *   *

Alvin followed Tony into the automatic elevator and when her finger pressed the button marked 'Penthouse' his lips pursed in a soundless whistle.

'Not bad,' he said.

'Of course, it's Carey's office too. He needs this kind of front. Lots of the big public relations men do it—convert town houses and all that.'

Her easy assurance made him look at her in a kind of wonder. A year ago a penthouse would have been as unreal to her as to him. He remembered the dingy Chicago rooming house where they had met and lived precariously. There was a bitter taste in his mouth as he acknowledged to himself that he could not have made the transition with the same ease or speed.

'Is your husband that important?' he asked.

'Not yet. But he's getting more prominent clients all the time.'

7

She unlocked the door onto a foyer from which a marble stairway curved grandly down to a lower floor. He had resolved not to reveal his feelings but in spite of himself he exclaimed, 'My God, a duplex!'

'You haven't seen anything yet.' With a rustle of the heavy corded-silk dress she whirled into his arms, kissed his cheek lightly and released herself before he could stir into action. 'Oh, it's fun, having you here. Showing you this, Alvin! I haven't had a single soul to show off to.'

When she was natural, he thought, she was just a sweet kid. He followed her into the big living-room which took up almost the whole top floor of the duplex. Even to Alvin's untutored eyes it was beautiful, a long L-shaped room with a fireplace and love seats, windows through which one saw the panorama of New York, a bar in the short end of the L. The furniture was modern without being eccentric, and the room was decorated in green and silver with a few splashes of scarlet in a pillow and in a painting over the empty grate.

'Did you plan this?'

She shook her head. 'No, Carey's first wife did the decorating. I left this room just as it was.'

'You say she divorced him?'

'Yes, but she's still around. She's Carey's business partner, Beatrice Comstock.'

Alvin whistled. 'That makes it nice.'

8

'Just lovely,' she said savagely. Then she laughed. 'Not that it really matters.' She tucked her hand under Alvin's arm. 'We'll mix a drink and then I'll show you the rest of the apartment.'

The rest of the top floor was taken up by a cloakroom, powder-room, electrified kitchen and butler's pantry.

'Carey entertains a lot,' Tony explained. 'Parties are an important part of his job. You get business that way, entertain the clients, even help to put them over by making the right contacts. All that sort of thing.'

She went back into the living-room and behind the bar. 'What will you have?'

'I never saw an array of bottles like that before,' Alvin admitted.

Tony laughed. 'For parties,' she said. 'And Carey likes to drink. He has such a lot of nerve strain in his job. I think it's better to make home as inviting as possible so that he'll do his drinking here instead of somewhere else.'

The wifely tone would hardly have deceived a Mongoloid idiot and Alvin asked curiously, 'What are you up to?'

'Nothing,' she said, wide eyed. 'Nothing at all. What do you want to drink?'

'I'll stick to gin. How about a Tom Collins?'

'Coming up,' she said and reached for a bottle with a practiced hand.

When she handed him his glass and picked up her own, she led the way out to a broad

9

terrace which extended around three sides of the building. She showed him her roses, the hedge, the dwarf trees, and a strip of lawn which was her pride. When she bent to pick a dead leaf from a plant Alvin chuckled.

'Maud Muller on a roof garden.'

'I keep pinching myself for fear I'll wake up,' she admitted. 'This is the way I want to live and I'll never give it up. Never.'

'Does anyone want you to?'

'Carey's family doesn't like me.'

'What kind of family does this Boy Wonder have?'

'Just a mother and sister. Margaret—that's my mother-in-law—isn't so bad. At least she's not the interfering kind. She runs a cheap hat shop on Lexington Avenue and doesn't expect Carey to support her. One of those ageless women. Fifty-five and still attractive.' Tony added grudgingly, 'She's really got something. Always polite to me, of course, but she wishes I was dead. And Carey's sister Jennie.' Tony laughed. 'Poor Jennie. She's a pain in the neck but pathetic, sort of. She's the dowdy, romantic kind, so anxious to be liked that you can't stand her.'

She leaned over the high railing and Alvin stood beside her, looking down at the East River and the lighted buildings.

'I've seen pictures like this but I never expected to see the real thing,' he declared. 'Imagine us here together.'

'Imagine us anywhere together,' she answered cryptically.

Her tone forced its way into his bemused mind and he gave her a swift, calculating look. 'You've picked a winner,' he said lightly.

She laid her cheek against his arm. 'I always do.'

With her face concealed, he could not see her expression, but he was aware that she was fencing just as he was, aware of the queer game they were playing with each other, and he felt a stir of excitement.

Tony went down the wide marble stairway, her long dress sweeping over the stairs. The lower floor contained a waiting-room in white leather and crimson, an office with paneled walls, a thick rug, easy chairs, and a table instead of a desk. The only indication that the room was used for business purposes was a small typewriter table, chair, and filing cabinets. Beyond there was a miniscule study in which there was a daybed.

'Used to be the secretary's office. Now it's Carey's bedroom,' Tony explained. 'That's the biggest change I've made here.' She opened the door of an untidy room with a four-poster bed, a fluffy dressing table cluttered with bottles, a chaise longue loaded with small cushions. The air was heavy with the odor of stale scent.

'That's all there is,' she said. 'You'd better go now. Carey might take it into his head to come home early for a change.'

'I'll call you tomorrow.' He saw the little frown that crossed her face and vanished.

'No,' she said. 'Don't call me here.'

'Why not? Just an old friend from Chicago.'

She sensed the change in him and she was careful. 'There's no use making trouble.'

'Don't tell me your husband is jealous.'

'Why not?' she said lazily. 'You are.'

He bent over her, one hand gripping her shoulder. 'You're a cruel little devil, Tony. Sometimes I wonder how long you'll get by with it.'

She did not bother to answer him.

'He doesn't come home evenings,' Alvin went on, 'but he sets you up like this and gives you emeralds. You must have plenty on him.'

'I have,' she said coolly.

His eyelids twitched. 'Tony, does he know where to get the stuff?'

He felt the involuntary jerk of her shoulder. 'No,' she began, and broke off abruptly.

'You don't often give anything away.' She heard the satisfaction in his tone. 'He doesn't know you use it, does he?'

She wanted to claw at his face but she forced herself to keep her voice casual. 'What of it?'

'I just wondered.' His tone was as cautious as her own. 'It's harder to get all the time. And expensive.'

'I can't help you out.' Watching his eyes, Tony added hastily, 'You know I would if I could, darling. But Carey doesn't give me much cash.'

'No?'

'No, he doesn't. He pays the bills and gives me an allowance and a darned small one.' The anger in her tone carried conviction.

'You could ask.'

Her ear caught his uncertainty and she was prompt to take advantage of it. 'Why should I?'

'Because I've got to have it,' he said simply. He wasn't fencing any longer. No threats. No demands. Just an unadorned statement. 'I've got to.'

Tony shook her head. 'He wouldn't give it to me.'

'You've got to ask. You owe me that much. You started me on it.'

'I hate a man who whines.'

Alvin straightened up. There were angry red marks where his fingers had gripped the soft flesh of her shoulder.

'I'm sorry,' she said. 'I didn't mean that. I'm just nervous, I guess.'

'You could say that to me! You've climbed up and kicked the ladder out from under you. Tony, you little fool, no one can get by with that. You were scared someone would see you talking to me when we met on Fifth Avenue. I'm too shabby for you. I'm just a bum.' His voice was getting high and excited. 'Well, that's tough because you can't shake me off like that.

13

You're going to see more of me.'

'If you think I'm going to give you money, you're wrong,' she said crisply. 'I've got expenses—big expenses.' There was a touch of bitterness in her voice.

'Too bad.'

'Alvin,' she screamed, 'you put that down!'

The emerald necklace gleamed in his hand and then he poured it into his pocket.

'You give that necklace back!'

For all his slight build he was able to hold her off easily. 'Buy it from me.' He turned toward the door and she ran after him.

'Give it back! Give it back!' Her face was distorted with rage.

'Ask Carey for another. If you've got so much on him, he'll come across.'

'Please, Alvin, please! You couldn't sell it. It's no good to you.'

'I've got to get more stuff. It's this or cash.'

'If you steal that necklace I'll call the police.'

'You wouldn't dare; you've got more to lose than I have.' He ran up the stairs and the outer door banged behind him.

For a long time Tony sat on the edge of the chaise longue, thinking furiously. Then she got up, emptied an ashtray, took the two highball glasses up to the kitchen where she rinsed them out and, after a final glance around, she lifted the telephone.

'I want a policeman,' she said steadily.

14

CHAPTER TWO

Carey sipped his port. California, he thought. The old skinflint. Even if it had been a vintage wine he would not have liked it. He belonged to a hard-liquor generation, but with practice he had learned his way around a winecard and he knew the right things to say.

He set down his glass and said the right things with the engaging smile that was usually sure fire. Tonight, however, it seemed to miss its target. Mrs Harrison Ives permitted her head to bend in a stately bow, the squire's lady acknowledging the cheers of the tenantry. That was the way it had been ever since his arrival, all during the interminable dinner. If his partner had not gallantly kept the conversation going, it would have bogged down altogether. The experience was a new and unpalatable one to Carey, who had discovered before he was twenty that he needed to make little effort where women were concerned.

Something had gone wrong with the evening. He had felt it from the first moment. Perhaps his hostess was a bit under the weather. There were big pouches under her eyes and a gray cast to her skin. She looked like a sick woman. Something must have happened to keep her in New York through the summer. At the beginning of the season she usually

15

headed for Newport.

The silence fell again and Beatrice, who showed signs of strain, began to discuss genealogy, a subject at which her hostess might be expected to shine. While the two women talked, Carey ran over in his mind the main lines of the campaign. It was good. It brought results. It was reasonably inexpensive as such things went. Now he regretted that he had not tacked on another ten thousand dollars. Mrs Harrison Ives's face had been a dead giveaway when he had mentioned—delicately, of course—the price. She was overwhelmed with relief. But what had she expected? He had told her last fall that the costs of the campaign would be lower a second year. It was a cinch to plant his stories once interest had been aroused.

She would sign, of course. It was all over but the shouting. And yet something was wrong. He would ask Beatrice afterwards whether she had noticed anything. If his imagination was getting out of hand—and he had imagined some queer things lately—he had better take steps. Strong steps. The time came when you had to stop fooling around.

'... almost no society today,' Mrs Harrison Ives was saying in her deep, authoritative voice. She never conversed. She made statements. 'Perhaps three hundred families in America who can be said to have any lineage. It makes one view the future with foreboding.'

16

There was no question about Mrs Harrison Ives's lineage. She knew her family tree down to the last twig, and with judicious pruning, a branch lopped off here, a weak one tied up there, and cement poured in to fortify the rotting trunk, it was a handsome tree. From its eminence she dominated society. Her position was unassailable and she accepted it with a full sense of humility, an awareness that she owed it a duty, that for its sweet rewards one must, like Portia's suitor, give and hazard all he has. Part priestess, part petty tyrant, she filled the position of social arbiter with immense dignity.

Occasionally there were speculations as to the source of her income. The late Harrison Ives had supplied blood of a satisfactory shade of blue but he had done little for the exchequer and he had faded out like watered ink.

His widow was fifty-five, a large woman with large, plain but serviceable features, the merest suggestion of a mustache, and a commanding manner. She would have made a superlative Madam Chairman if she had cared to devote time to committees. As it happened, she had no time for committees. Only Carey Walker and his discreet partner, Beatrice Comstock, knew how she spent her leisure hours. And half the time Carey did not believe it.

'Every time I look at her,' he once told Beatrice, 'I know it's impossible. That woman simply can't be writing the most erotic novels in America today. The thing's fantastic. When

I send out a story on the mystery woman I think the biggest mystery of all is that she could write them. Lydia Longstreet! Lydia! What is the dowager's first name? She was probably christened Mrs Harrison Ives.'

'Her first name is Amanda,' Beatrice told him, 'and it is women like that who write erotic novels.'

The sales of the most recent Lydia Longstreet opus, a sizzling number entitled *The Reluctant Lovers*, had reached the half-million mark. Mrs Ives had been delighted. Ordinarily, her novels would have had a small under-the-counter sale, but with the Walker-Comstock agency on the job, they were a public scandal. Reviewers sneered, less successful novelists were bitter, and the movie companies were outbidding each other and wondering how to get past the Johnston office. People who had not bought a book since *Forever Amber* were stampeding into the book stores, expressing moral indignation and wondering why the publisher brought out such stuff. They hadn't dreamed, until they just happened to glance at it, that the book was like that. And they all talked about it, the only sure-fire way to sell books. On the whole, Carey thought the agency had done a swell job.

Almost invariably it was he who handled the women clients but it was Beatrice who knew how to deal with Mrs Harrison Ives. One of the most delightful qualities about his ex-wife was that her surprises were never exhausted. Age could not wither her nor custom stale her infinite variety. Carey was pleased at the ease with which the quotation had come to him. As a rule he did not think in literary allusions. He must tell Beatrice. No, on second thought, he must not tell Beatrice. She had always been touchy about being five years older than he. And Tony never let slip a chance to mention Beatrice's age. Tony—this was no time to think of Tony. Time enough for that later.

Carey wondered what it was that gave his ex-wife the quality people call charm. She was not pretty. Her mouth was too big for her thin face. So were her eyes, which were accentuated by the winged black brows and black hair that set off the creamy pallor of her skin. The small, high-bridged nose, like the carriage of her head, made her appear haughty.

Carey leaned forward and Beatrice deftly brought the subject back by easy stages from genealogy to society to the masses to public opinion and so to the pending contract. It was curious that they had always known each other's mental processes, as though tuned in on the same wave length. Beatrice said there was a name for it, extrasensory perception.

She handed Carey his cue and waited for him to take the lead. He began to talk now. He had a persuasive voice, an easy manner, and a beautifully articulated body whose immense vitality had much to do with his success. He

19

was tall, with medium-brown hair, a rather rough-hewn face almost as dark as his hair from on-the-cuff sojourns in Florida, supplemented by a sun lamp. He talked with intensity and sincerity. Sincerity was Carey's watchword. People always responded to sincerity.

Well, almost always. Mrs Harrison Ives listened and nodded her head at the end of each paragraph. But when the pen was in her hand, hovering over the dotted line, she hesitated. The flabby skin of her jaw line quivered.

'Mr Walker,' she said in her deep voice, 'I'd like to have another clause in this contract.'

Beatrice lifted her head alertly, like a dog scenting danger.

'It is the same contract you had last year,' Carey reminded her. 'Except that the cost to you is lower.'

The dowager tapped the pen against the square palm of her left hand. 'I don't like to mince words. I am a direct woman. My career is essential to me. It is practically my only source of income. But a woman in my social position cannot afford a shadow of scandal. Rather than incur such a risk I would give up writing altogether.'

'But what risk can there possibly be?' Beatrice asked. 'After all, only the three of us know that you are Lydia Longstreet.'

'Only the three of us.' Mrs Harrison Ives's tired eyes searched Carey's handsome-ugly

20

face and Beatrice's clever one like an explorer surveying hostile terrain. 'None the less, I want a clause automatically canceling this contract if my name should ever be associated publicly with my work.'

Carey glanced at Beatrice who replied with the merest flicker of her eyelids. There was a polite fiction between them that it was Carey who made the decisions.

'Of course,' he said pleasantly, 'we'll have the clause typed in tomorrow and send the revised contracts to you for signature.'

'No. There is a typewriter in my study if you would care to use it.'

Beatrice rose, a tall, slim woman, and followed her hostess, walking down the room as though she owned it.

Carey stood at the window of Mrs Harrison Ives's apartment looking out at Central Park. In a few moments she returned and sat down heavily. She did not speak nor did Carey move. The silence was unbroken until Beatrice returned, her long skirt whispering as she crossed the room.

*   *   *

When they came out of the cool building onto the street, it seemed to Beatrice that the street lights were flickering. Or perhaps her eyes were tired. She must go back to her exercises. If she were careful, she could put off wearing glasses

21

a little longer. They aged a woman.

'All our best clients are out of town for the summer,' Carey had pointed out a month earlier. 'We might as well close up. New York is really unbearable in July. Tony and I could fly out to San Francisco so I'd have a chance to talk to Bellows face to face. Only way to get anywhere with that bird. And you,' he had had the grace to hesitate, 'I suppose you've kept the place in the White Mountains.'

She had not replied, 'You know I was always afraid to stay there alone.' Instead, she had insisted, 'We can't close up. Summer is just the time to launch the Harrison Ives campaign, and we've got to have everything lined up for the George woman by fall. And there's Miles Aldrich. A few weeks of work and we could have him signed, sealed, and delivered.'

'I don't want the Aldrich account,' Carey had said with the unaccountable stubbornness that accompanied his drinking bouts. 'I've told you that before.'

Because she was not a woman who abandoned a cherished project without a struggle, she had tried to reason with him. 'But Carey, it's a cinch. We can build him as a great humanitarian. I have a honey of a campaign planned. Wait until you see what I've mapped out.'

'I don't want any part in it. I can't stand the guy.' His voice was sullen, his eyes bloodshot. Little by little his good looks were being blurred by puffiness. It did not seem possible a man could change so much in a few months.

There was nothing to be done with him when he was in this condition, but because she was tenacious she had gone on doggedly, 'A public relations counsel doesn't have to like his clients. Anyhow, you might as well get used to Miles Aldrich. You may have him in your family one of these days.'

'You really think that he is going to marry Jennie?' Carey shook his head. 'I don't get it. My sister is a good kid but I can't see any man falling for her. How the hell did that Y.W.C.A. strain get into my family?'

It was unusual for Beatrice to lose her temper with Carey but she had answered sharply, 'Don't be a fool and let your prejudices get the best of you! A multi-millionaire brother-in-law will do you no harm at all.'

Carey had smiled at her and he had an engaging smile. 'All right,' he had capitulated. 'You're the doctor. We stay in town. We sweat and strain. We earn an honest dollar.'

'And anyhow,' she had lied. 'I don't mind the heat.'

So she had no one but herself to blame if she had let herself in for the heat wave. Just the same, it annoyed her to hear Carey say brightly as they emerged from Mrs Harrison Ives's apartment, 'Is it my fevered imagination or do I detect a breeze? Let's sample the Scotch at one of the sidewalk cafés on Central Park South.'

For a moment Beatrice hesitated. The last thing Carey needed at this point was Scotch. It was a wonder Mrs Harrison Ives had not noticed how heavily he had been drinking. If he went on this way much longer he'd be needing a cure. She wondered whether there would be any use in saying so and decided against it.

At the St Moritz they each ordered a highball and while they waited, Carey tucked the contracts away in his pocket.

For some reason neither of them was anxious to discuss Mrs Harrison Ives. Beatrice pushed back her hair with a weary gesture.

'What weather! You're really mad to be giving that cocktail party tomorrow.'

'There's always a breeze on the terrace,' Carey pointed out. 'Anyhow, it's good for business. Let the clients look at each other and be impressed.'

'Speaking of clients,' Beatrice said, 'I've got a new prospect. John Harland, the man who wrote *Man's Worst Enemy*.'

Carey considered, his eyes thoughtful. 'That might be a hard nut to crack. Scientific stuff, isn't it?'

'But the man himself is wonderful,' Beatrice said eagerly. 'Knee-deep in excitement all the time.'

'Where did you come across him?'

'He was a neighbor when I was a girl of

fifteen.' She figured rapidly. Twenty-five years ago. She winced as she thought of that passage of time. 'I've followed his career. Not much of it reaches the newspapers but old friends have written me. He's carried on the most extraordinary number of careers. He—'

'We haven't much time for new clients,' Carey said huffily, and Beatrice thought in amazement: Why, he's jealous. 'The Harrison Ives stuff will keep us busy. This has been a nice evening's work. But, do you know, Trix, for a moment she had me worried. I thought she wouldn't sign.'

Beatrice took the profferred cigarette. Her navy blue dinner dress was plain but the wide sleeves that hung over her hands made each of her rare gestures dramatic. Her narrow face seemed haggard for all the care she bestowed on it, and just now it was stripped of its usual assurance.

'Mrs Harrison Ives didn't want to sign that contract. Couldn't you see that?'

'But why? We've done a damn good job for her. She has nothing to kick about.'

Beatrice traced a line along the table with a fingertip. 'She thinks she has.'

'Then why didn't she say so?'

Beatrice watched him as she replied. 'She made it clear enough. She thinks we intend to double-cross her. We are the only ones who know the identity of Lydia Longstreet. Therefore, if it gets out—'

There was nothing but bewilderment to be read in Carey's face. Beatrice longed to shake him, to say, 'Be real.'

'The old girl's balmy,' he said indifferently. 'Why should we cut our own throats? I could feel there was something in the air. She was in a queer mood. If I spoke to her she jumped.'

'I think,' Beatrice said slowly, 'she's the kind of woman who wouldn't stop short of murder to keep people from knowing about the Lydia Longstreet side of her life. She couldn't survive ridicule. Her social position is a kind of cult with her.'

Carey was not impressed. 'What's she worrying about? Her little secret is in safe hands.'

Beatrice flicked her unsmoked cigarette over the hedge and watched it roll across the sidewalk until the heel of a pedestrian ground out the glowing tip. She caught her lip between her teeth. Then she said, 'She's afraid of you, Carey.'

Carey's laugh was one of his finest assets. It was infectious but Beatrice did not smile. 'Why is she afraid? What have you been up to?'

'Oh, for God's sake, Trix!' he exclaimed irritably. 'I thought we could have a pleasant, friendly drink for once—'

'Why can't we?'

'Let's not quarrel,' Carey pleaded with his winning smile. 'Not tonight. It's been one of those days and I need this quiet time with you.'

'Right you are,' Beatrice said briskly. She raised her glass. 'Happy days.'

Carey slammed his glass down so hard that the ashtray jumped. A vein in his temple began to swell. Beatrice could see it throb.

'Watch that temper, Carey,' she said, trying to speak lightly. The worst of being five years older was that she never dared give advice for fear she would sound maternal.

'Why do you say that? My temper hasn't victimized you, has it?'

'It's going to get you into trouble one of these days. Bad trouble.'

'Trix the soothsayer!' He raised his glass. 'To crime.'

'To another fat contract. Without crime. Miles Aldrich as first choice.'

'That's the big thing I had to tell you tonight,' he said, 'Miles Aldrich is engaged to Jennie. She called me this morning, positively stuttering with joy.' He shook his head. 'If anyone had told me ten years ago I'd have an Aldrich for a brother-in-law—just a small-town boy making good. That's me.'

'Whoa,' she protested. 'Aren't you taking too much credit? After all, you aren't marrying the man. Your sister is.'

'And I'll never understand it,' he admitted. 'Jennie landing a whale with a—bent pin on a string.'

'You underrate Jennie. You always did, because she isn't your type.' This came

27

dangerously close to the Forbidden Topic and Beatrice added hastily, 'Why do you dislike Miles Aldrich so much?'

'I do not like you, Doctor Fell.'

'That's going to be a successful marriage, Carey.'

'Oh, successful—yes.' There was an undercurrent of distaste in his voice.

'What I mean by successful,' she said, 'isn't what you mean. I think those two love each other.'

Carey's lips were white. 'First time I ever knew you to hit below the belt.'

The Forbidden Topic stared them in the face. By dint of long practice Beatrice was prepared to skirt it. Instead, she said in a rush, 'Then why did you marry Tony? If it wasn't love, what was it? Infatuation? Her youth? Her tactics? Did you *want* to marry her?'

'It's getting late,' Carey said, 'and tomorrow is another day. Another happy day. God's in his heaven, all's right with the world.'

'I wish you'd drop *Bartlett's Quotations*.'

'Right you are,' he said amiably. 'Shall we have another little drink? No, we shall not have another little drink. We shall be as sober as a judge. Do you think judges have any fun? Judge not that ye be not judged.'

Beatrice pushed back her chair angrily and Carey got up. He paid the check and laid her wrap over her shoulders.

'For a wonder, here's an empty cab,' he said.

28

He helped her in and closed the door.

CHAPTER THREE

In her little, one-price hatshop on Lexington Avenue, Margaret Walker picked up a shapeless handful of silk, shook it, gave it a few deft twists, and then pulled it carefully over her hair. It looked like the one she had seen for twelve-fifty in the shop on Madison. Silly, she told her reflection in the mirror, but smart.

It was also becoming. Her charming face refused to age. The widening streak of white in her brown hair struck her friends as an amusing idiosyncrasy. People declined to accept the idea that Margaret Walker could grow old.

As far as she was concerned, she rarely thought about it. Now and then she took herself to task for her incurable frivolity. The mother of two grown children, a son thirty-five and a daughter twenty-five, had no right to be frivolous, particularly when her children took life so hard. For them it was something they had to conquer. Margaret never tried to conquer anything. While Carey attempted to outwit life and trick it into giving him what he wanted; and Jennie, strenuous and awkward, tried to take it by assault; Margaret accepted it, half wryly, half amused.

One of her more sober moods was upon her now, and she had stayed in her shop after the clerks had gone so that she could have a few minutes to herself. It was time she thought things out and she had to do it in her own way, which, being Margaret, was highly individual.

In the glass she looked at the woman other people saw when they talked to Margaret Walker: a brisk, bright-eyed woman with a girl's mischievous smile. She was fifty-five and looked ten years younger, but there were times when she felt sixty. Not often, but sometimes after hours of standing, being polite to customers. Like today.

Just the same, Margaret nodded emphatically at her image, I'm not going to give up the shop. I always said I wouldn't be a burden to my children and I mean it. I wouldn't let Carey support me and I'm not going to let Jennie do it. Not even with all that Aldrich money. Poor Jennie.

Now why, she asked herself in astonishment, do I say poor Jennie? Anyone in his right mind would think she's the luckiest girl in the world. Miles is the kind of man a dutiful mother would work her fingers to the bone to land for her daughter.

It felt good to be sitting down and to be alone. No customers to flatter or appease. No clerks to watch. She got more tired than she used to. Better not let Jennie guess. Jennie was so emphatic about things. She always did something about them and what she did was usually wrong.

Margaret absently gave the hat a little touch so that it tilted to one side at a rakish angle and considered her children. Why was it, she thought, that she could not take her children for granted as other mothers did? They astonished her.

How had she, of all people, managed to produce them? Carey, who had such charm that her heart melted when she thought of him because he was so much like his father, and yet he had a driving ambition that his happy-go-lucky father would never have understood. All that he had, all he was, became tools to help his relentless drive. Even his charm—he used that too. At least, until a few months ago. Now the drive seemed to have gone out of him. His eyes were dull, his mouth was slackening. He was beginning to look like an habitual drinker. There's nothing so hard, Margaret thought, as loving a person and having to stand aside, to do nothing, to keep hands off. Her hands clenched and she looked down at them curiously and then relaxed the fingers one by one.

And Jennie. Wistful Jennie who would have sold her soul for charm. If she didn't try so hard to make people like her, Margaret thought, they couldn't help seeing how nice she really is. She doesn't understand that you can't force liking; that it just happens.

31

Jennie, Margaret told herself firmly, is a much nicer person than I am. She's so earnest. She's never frivolous about serious things. She and Miles will do so much good in the world. Margaret's heart sank as she contemplated all the good they would do. It's awful, she thought, to be bored by your own son-in-law. I don't seem to like the people my children marry. I didn't like Beatrice Comstock, although at least she didn't bore me. And she saw through Carey just as I do and loved him anyhow.

There was probably a good deal to be said for Beatrice, especially when one remembered Tony, the little wretch! Destroying Carey bit by bit and jabbing at Jennie all the time with Jennie never knowing how to defend herself.

Someone was tapping persistently on the locked door of the shop and Margaret saw a man's face pressed against the glass as he tried to peer in. Oh, dear, she thought in distress, not David. I simply can't cope with David tonight. If he thinks I am going to take him home for dinner he is mistaken. It is bad enough dealing with the people my children marry. I am not responsible for the ones they turn down.

She opened the door and admitted a red-headed young man with a good chin and freckles sprinkled across a shapely nose. Because his shoulders were so broad, he seemed shorter than he really was.

'Hello, David!'

'I just happened to be passing and saw the light.' He noticed her hat. 'Don't let me keep you though,' he said with false cheerfulness, 'if you were leaving.'

He looked so dejected that Margaret said quickly, 'I have all the time in the world.' Anyhow, she told herself, no one would mind if dinner was a little late. And she simply couldn't send him away when he looked like that. He shoved his hat on the back of his head. There were shadows under his eyes as though he had not been sleeping well. Oh, the young, she thought; the pitiful young. And she said much more warmly than she had intended, 'We haven't seen you for weeks, David. We've missed you.'

'Yaah,' he snorted derisively. 'I'll bet Jennie never even noticed that I was staying away.'

Being a woman who was hampered by a truthful nature—except when selling hats, and no one could sell hats and be truthful—Margaret could think of no soothing or reassuring reply.

'Look, Mrs Walker.' David leaned forward with an impetuous gesture that knocked two hats on the floor. Margaret swooped them up, shook them, removed the ribbon affair, and tried them on at different angles. They really were awful.

'I know,' David said doggedly, 'a reporter doesn't make a big salary. But do you think money is the whole thing?'

33

'Heavens, no!'

'Can you see what this Aldrich bird has except money?'

Frankly, Margaret could not, but she was loyal to Jennie. 'He's a very nice person.'

'He's an exploiter of the poor.'

In spite of herself, Margaret could not prevent the mischievous smile from flashing across her face. 'Fiddlesticks!' she retorted. 'You simply can't make a villain out of Miles. He has the soul of a Baptist preacher.'

David's laugh had a hollow sound. 'Aldrich the humanitarian,' he muttered. Then he dropped the histrionics and asked simply, 'Is Jennie going to marry him?'

'Yes,' Margaret said with equal directness. 'I'm sorry, David.'

'Sorry it's Miles or sorry it's not me?'

She patted his hand because she could not answer his question. All the angry color had faded from his face and he was so white that her heart was sick with pity for him.

I'm glad I'm not young, she thought. Even for the sake of being in love again. Especially for that. Only the young are resilient enough to bear that anguish.

'I've got to run along and cook dinner for my brood. Will you come? We'd all be glad to have you.'

'No, thanks,' he said. 'I'd just be in the way.' He got up and his elbow sent a hand mirror crashing to the floor.

'Oh, David!' she expostulated. 'Seven years of bad luck.'

'That's not the mirror,' he said grimly. 'That is Miles Aldrich entering the family. He has blighted everything he touched. And everybody. You know about his brother, don't you? Ask him some time to tell you about his brother. Well, I'll be shoving on.' He added defiantly, 'And give Jennie my love.'

*　　*　　*

If only, Margaret thought as she thrust her key into the lock, if only Jennie hasn't started dinner. It is so much easier when Jennie isn't being helpful. She opened the door and cried out in delight, 'Carey!'

He picked her up, hugged her, and set her down, eying her critically. 'You are wearing one of your own hats again,' he said. 'When are you going to spend a little money on yourself?'

'Beatrice made you clothes conscious,' she commented. Oh, dear, she thought, why do I always say the wrong thing? She looked at her son with a pride she tried in vain to conceal. He was outrageously attractive. 'I'm so glad you came early,' she said. 'Jennie will be pleased. She wants you and Miles to know each other better. Didn't Tony come with you?'

Carey's face and voice emptied of expression as they always did when he discussed his wife.

'She couldn't. She was a bit under the

35

weather and went to bed. She's terribly sorry.'

In her relief that Tony would not be there to spoil things for Jennie, Margaret didn't care why she had stayed away. Though I'd have thought, she told herself, Tony wouldn't miss a chance to meet a man like Miles. It just shows how unjust I am. And anyhow, it only postpones the evil moment.

'Carey,' she said aloud, 'we ought to have some kind of party for Jennie, to celebrate her engagement. Would Tony mind if you gave it in your penthouse? It would seem more festive.'

'What are we waiting for?' Carey said promptly. 'Give me your list tonight and we'll telephone Jennie's friends and tie it in with the cocktail party I'm giving tomorrow for a few of our clients. And I'll make the announcement myself—with flourishes.'

His tone warmed her heart. So many things are wrong, Margaret thought, but the affection Carey and Jennie have for each other is completely right, strong and enduring.

'Leave the details to me,' Carey added. 'If you read the right columnists you'd know I am considered a very good party man. You get the gal properly dressed. If you don't watch her, she'll come looking like the White Queen. And don't give her a hat from your shop.' He felt for his billfold and stopped her protest. 'This is for Jennie.'

'Come out to the kitchen while I get things

started,' Margaret said, 'and tell me all the news.'

'What's the use of having a tycoon in the family if you do the cooking?' Carey protested. 'You are tired.'

'Not very. And Miles does enjoy my cooking. He loves simple things. In that huge place of his there wasn't much family life, you know.'

'You're breaking my heart.'

Speaking of family life reminded Margaret of what David Morehouse had said. Something about Miles's brother. Of course, David always saw Miles in the worst possible light, not merely on Jennie's account but because, as a self-respecting radical, he opposed the very existence of people like Miles.

'Do you know anything about Miles's brother?' she asked idly. 'The one who died?'

Carey flung up the windows. 'That's better,' he said. 'It was stuffy in here. What's that you said?'

'Miles's brother. Did you ever hear anything about him?'

'The Aldriches and the Walkers,' Carey pointed out, 'have not moved in the same circles up to now. Why do you ask?'

'I don't know—something David More-house said today. You remember David?'

'That red-headed flame-eater who has been hanging around Jennie? What did he tell you?'

'He's upset about Jennie and Miles, of course. He's devoted to Jennie.'

Carey laughed. 'Fancy our Jennie being the *femme fatale*. I'll fix us some drinks. I don't suppose we dare touch the demon rum after Aldrich gets here. I warn you, Mom, fond as I am of Jennie, I am not going to take the pledge.'

Margaret defended her prospective son-in-law half heartedly. 'Miles isn't that bad. He always takes one drink just to show that he's not fanatical about it. He isn't really narrow. Just moderate. And so well meaning.' She tossed off the hat, ran a hand through her hair—fortunately it had a natural curl—and trotted into the kitchen.

The door opened with a bang and Jennie came romping in. She was ten years younger than Carey and looked a great deal like him, the same large frame, the same roughhewn features. She was big and breezy, with a boarding-school mind and energy which she could not exhaust by her classes in athletics for underprivileged girls. As usual, she looked as though she had dressed in the dark. Her mother would have made a smart dress of an old curtain. Put Jennie in a Lanvin model and it would look like something she had run up at home.

She flung herself exuberantly at Carey and he kissed her. 'I was afraid you'd be too busy to come!'

'Not when my only sister gets herself engaged. Where's the lucky man?'

'He'll be along soon. Oh, Carey, I can hardly believe it's happened.'

He grinned at her. 'You must like the guy.'

Jennie never understood teasing. 'You'll like him too when you know him, Carey. He's so—fine. I realize,' she said, trying to be just, 'you're prejudiced because his father wasn't all he should have been.'

'His father,' Carey informed her, 'was a coldblooded buccaneer if there ever was one. But at least the old horse thief collected those millions Miles is doling out to worthy causes.'

'He does a lot of good,' Jennie defended him.

'Don't forget the home team,' Carey said. 'Drop a hint at the right moment that Walker-Comstock can build up his publicity.' As she looked distressed he laughed. 'Forget it. If the guy wants his name tacked on his good deeds, it's all in the spirit of fun.'

'You don't understand,' Jennie said earnestly. 'Miles knows what people think of his father and he felt terrible about his brother Graham being a spectacular playboy and dying the way he did. He wants to make the Aldrich name respected. Oh, and that reminds me. Don't mention Graham. It upsets Miles.'

'Any more instructions before I meet the great man?'

'Don't be cross, Carey.' The doorbell rang and Jennie exclaimed, 'There he is now and I'm

39

not ready. Let him in, will you?'

Being born to the purple had not prevented Miles Aldrich from looking like one of his more obscure clerks. He was the invisible man; nature had designed him for background material, a part of the faceless crowd. He was so negative, Carey had declared the first time he met him, that he turned it into a positive quality. He was Carey's age but he had never looked young nor would he ever look old. He had an austere face, with hair parted in the middle and already growing thin. He wore rimless glasses over light eyes, and a neat smile revealed even teeth.

He held out his hand. 'Hello, Carey.'

'Come in, Aldrich.'

'Miles. It's all in the family now.'

'So I hear. Well, the best to you both. Every happiness and all that. Jennie is a good kid—'

'You can rest assured,' Miles said solemnly, 'I'll do everything I can to make her happy. In my family we marry for keeps.' He looked embarrassed. 'Oh, I'm sorry. I shouldn't have said that.'

'No harm done,' Carey said easily. 'This occasion calls for a drink.'

'Why, thanks, Carey, but I think I'll wait until we can all have one together.'

'Right. But if you don't mind, I'll have a quick one now.'

'Oh, of course. I don't dream of dictating to other people what they should do. I just find it

40

best for myself. Keeps my brain clearer.'

Carey went out into the kitchen where Margaret was peeling potatoes and took down a bottle of rye. 'Thirsty work,' he told her in a whisper, mixed them each a drink, set hers on the floor beside her chair where it would be out of sight, winked at her and went back to the other room.

'Isn't your wife joining us?' Miles asked politely. 'I looked forward to meeting her.'

'Not tonight. She's feeling shaky and decided to stay in bed.' He glanced toward the kitchen door and lowered his voice. 'I went out to see a client last night and came home to find the place crawling with policemen. Well, one policeman anyhow.'

Miles gave a little exclamation of concern.

'Seems my wife was asleep when someone broke into the place. He scared the life out of her. I didn't mention it to Mom. She might worry.'

'I hope you lost nothing.'

Carey took a long pull at his drink. 'Nothing of any value,' he said.

CHAPTER FOUR

John Harland, looking like an elegant but emaciated shadow, paused for a moment in the doorway, looking around the crowded living-room of Carey Walker's penthouse. White hair framed a face as narrow as a knife blade and with a profile that was equally sharp. In fact, the man was so thin that he seemed to be all profile. Under beetling eyebrows were deep-socketed blue eyes.

If anyone had told him that his pronounced leanness, his heavy white hair, his deep-set eyes distinguished him in any group he would have been chagrined. He regarded himself so completely as an onlooker at life that he was always surprised to discover his own visibility.

The reputation and acclaim that had followed the unexpected success of *Man's Worst Enemy* amused him and he regarded them as strange phenomena of an unpredictable public. Harland had vanity but it was not of a personal nature. His appearance did not interest him, nor its effect on others. He was not concerned with surfaces but with the stresses and tensions that lay beneath them.

Before being engulfed in a party he liked to take his bearings. This party was not what he had expected. Obviously, it was not a success although he could not, at the moment, determine what was wrong. He tucked the impression away in his mind for further consideration. The room itself was charming but the party was set in a different key. Observing the uniformed maids, the bartender busy with his array of bottles, the elaborate platters of hors d'oeuvres, the massed flowers, he was reminded irresistibly of Jane Carlyle's tart comment on being shown over the home of some *nouveau riche*—'How expensive!'

None of these people seemed to belong together. They did not circulate, remaining in tight, exclusive groups that gave one another swift, appraising glances.

The oddest group of all stood at the open door leading to the terrace: a handsome woman of fifty, a streamlined job, clutching the arm of a girl with a triangular face and a body which deserved the second glance every man gave it. But it was the girl's face which attracted Harland's attention. There was a dark swelling under one eye, another at the curve of her jaw. She was attempting without success to extricate herself from the grasp of the Streamlined Job, who continued to hold her like the Ancient Mariner.

A woman came to meet Harland, both hands outstretched in greeting, with a wide, warm smile that transformed her from a sophisticated woman to a charming one.

'Beatrice!' he exclaimed in a pleasant baritone that was unexpectedly young.

'How did you know?' she asked. 'It's been so long.' It was curious that he did not seem any older to the woman of forty than he had to the girl of fifteen. She had regarded him then as ageless. Now she realized that he could have been no more than thirty. 'I've changed a lot,' she added.

'Your eyes are still the same, Beatrice. Still hungry eyes. I'm glad to see you.' He had a warmth of manner that would charm a bird off a tree, she thought. 'When your invitation came I couldn't resist it. I've often wondered what happened to you.'

'Flatterer!'

'No,' Harland said tranquilly. 'I never flatter. But I don't like unsolved problems. They keep nagging at me.' He turned his extraordinarily blue eyes on Beatrice. No one she had ever known gave the same impression of bestowing his whole attention. That, she supposed, was why he had been able to pursue so many fields of interest. He had a capacity for complete absorption in the thing he was doing.

'I want you to myself,' she said impulsively, 'before you get snared by a lot of people.' She signaled a maid and when he had a drink she said, 'Let's go down to the office where we can talk.'

Her dress was dark, tailored and smart, her only adornment being huge gold earrings shaped like clock faces with numbers but no hands. They called attention to the gold flecks in the huge eyes which were her one beauty.

'Unusual,' Harland commented.

'I think they are amusing.' Beatrice turned to wave a greeting to a newcomer.

'That's not the word I would have used. A bit macabre.'

She looked at him quickly. ''You don't miss

much.'

'I know a clock with no hands means death. Hardly the festive touch.'

'Oh, I don't know. They provoke comment and that's always a help, particularly at a party like this,' and she looked around at the set groups with a kind of comic despair.

'I've been wondering what was wrong with it' he admitted.

'It didn't jell. We tried to combine business with pleasure.'

'And which am I?'

'You were supposed to be business,' Beatrice admitted frankly. 'I'm full of plans for exploiting you. But I suspect you are going to be pleasure too.'

She slipped her hand under his arm. 'Come down to the office with me. Take your drink along.'

Without protest he followed her down the broad, marble staircase, as thin, as unsubstantial as a shadow, but his pace was quick and nervous and his eyes amused.

She looked at him suspiciously. 'What are you laughing at?'

'I wasn't laughing,' he protested. 'I was wondering.'

'You haven't changed a bit!' Her face was much younger when she smiled. Happiness, Harland thought, would make her a fascinating woman, softening, perhaps obliterating, the tense lines at the corner of her mouth, like faint parentheses, lines that in a few years would deepen.

She led him through a white and crimson waiting-room on the lower floor of the duplex and into the office. 'Do you remember,' she asked, 'how you used to teach me to work puzzles and figure out codes and ciphers? We spent simply hours on them.'

Hours, he recalled, that he had taken grudgingly from his work because the lonely child had aroused his compassion. The aunt and uncle who were bringing her up were kindly people who did their duty, but the little girl had been avid for affection. How many afternoons he had found her on his doorstep, her manner casual, her eyes pleading. She asked nothing but she would wait tenaciously until he noticed her. And knowing that she would not go away, that she would stay until he capitulated, he would put aside his work and take out a puzzle to amuse her.

'I still like puzzles,' he said. 'I have one now. Who's the girl with the pin-up body and the battered face, and why does she come to a party looking like that?'

'She is your hostess,' Beatrice said. 'Her name is Tony Walker—Mrs Carey Walker—and she is my ex-husband's new wife.'

'But I understood I was your guest.'

'So you are. It's not complicated really. Carey Walker and I were business partners as well as husband and wife. We got divorced and

46

he re-married, but we are still business partners. I don't live here but I work here. You are now—if it interests you—in the office of the highly successful firm of public relations counselors, Walker-Comstock.'

Harland gave a little chortle of pleasure. 'That reminds me,' he said. 'I was looking up the word counsel the other day. Do you know how Webster defines it? "Archaic: the exercise of deliberate judgment." Now start at the beginning and tell me all about yourself.'

What curious eyes he had, she thought. Ageless in an aging face. Young and clear and shining. But she saw nothing of him in his eyes, only a reflection of herself. And it was not a pose. He was incapable of posing, not because he was ingenuous but because he did not think it worth the bother.

'Where do I start?' she asked obediently.

'With this business of yours. I take it you and your—partner make a good team.'

'We do. The business is thriving. And,' she added, 'there is no hard feeling.'

Harland rubbed his long nose thoughtfully with a forefinger. 'It is fortunate that Carey's wife does not mind.'

'Tony? Why should she? We are all perfectly civilized.'

'No one,' Harland chided her, 'is perfectly civilized. You are an intelligent woman. You know a situation like that holds seeds of trouble.'

'Yes, it does,' she agreed unexpectedly. 'But not the kind of trouble you mean.'

'What kind do I mean?'

'Emotional complications, of course. But Carey and I are all through. I'm not jealous of Tony. And yet there is something wrong, John.' She stamped out her cigarette with nervous fingers. 'Tony might as well have dropped from the moon so far as her past is concerned. She's the girl from nowhere. She chatters all the time but she never drops a word about where she came from or her family or anything. She's too—careful.'

'Doesn't Carey know anything about her past?'

Beatrice shrugged slim shoulders. 'If he does,' she said dryly, 'he keeps it to himself.'

'What's worrying you?' Harland asked gently.

'That girl is more than a common trouble-maker. She is evil.'

Harland looked at her, a graceful woman, cool and poised except for the smoldering eyes. 'You are a decorative creature,' he said. 'I like the way you set off this room.' He added quietly, 'Has Carey been complaining?'

'Of course not.'

'Does he seem to be unhappy with her?'

'He would hardly discuss that with me. Our relations are purely business. But Carey is going to pieces. He is drinking heavily and it is doing him no good. It is doing the business no good either. And Tony encourages his drinking. I've watched her. And I'm not going to draw up a chair tamely and watch my partner being turned into a dipsomaniac.'

'Let it alone, Beatrice. Let it alone, my dear.'

'Let sleeping female dogs lie?' she asked. 'Or should I say—Let Carey go to the dogs?'

He went on as though she had not spoken. 'And if I were you, I'd give up the business. Clear out altogether.'

There was shocked disbelief in Beatrice's face followed by fierce protest. 'But it's mine as much as it is his. Carey and I built it together.'

'What do you propose to do?'

'I want to find out the truth about that girl before she does too much damage.' The tension died out of her face and she leaned forward, bringing her hands together with a swift, graceful gesture. 'That's enough about me. Let me tell you about a plan I have for you, John. Carey and I could make you one of the most spectacular figures in America.'

Harland's eyes twinkled. 'You frighten me.'

'It would be wonderful. The things you've done, John! In your quiet, unobtrusive way you've had a terrific life. Look at that work you did in Germany before we got into the war—'

'How did you find out about that?' he interrupted.

She made a vague gesture. 'I have contacts. And the way you stopped that State Department scandal—'

'You have too many contacts,' he said grimly.

'These things can't be hidden,' she told him. 'Someone was bound to know. And you saved old Mrs Jenkins from being declared incompetent by her son-in-law. I want people to appreciate you. Why, I could get you radio interviews, maybe a movie short, a television re-enactment of one of your cases, or whatever you call them, syndicated news stories—with pictures.' She stood leaning against a chair, the supple grace of her body emphasized by the lines of her dress, the huge eyes burning in her thin face. She was alive, dynamic, intense. Harland felt as though he were talking to a sheet of flame.

'You fascinate me,' he said. 'But my immediate need is for another drink.'

Their eyes met and she laughed. 'I'll let you off this time,' she capitulated. 'But I'm not going to give you up, John. Nature never intended you to bloom in the shade like a violet.'

They were starting up the marble stairs when Harland's eye was caught by a slight movement. Beatrice followed his gaze and saw the door at the end of the hall closing. She looked at it, a frown between her delicate eyebrows.

'That's Tony's room,' she said, 'and I know she's upstairs. I wonder—go on up, will you, John? I'll join you in just a moment.'

Swiftly and silently she went down the hall and opened the door. The Streamlined Job was standing at Tony's dressing table, rummaging through a drawer. She whirled around as she caught sight of Beatrice.

'Mrs George!' Beatrice said in surprise.

'Oh,' Mrs George said. 'You startled me. I thought—'

'Are you looking for something?' Beatrice asked as quietly as though she were accustomed to finding guests searching the apartment. Even in her astonishment she did not forget that Mrs George was a client.

'A needle and thread,' Mrs George said. 'I've torn a strap off my slip.'

'What a nuisance. I doubt whether Mrs Walker has such a thing. We'll ask the maid. She does the mending.'

'Sorry to be such a bother.'

'Not at all.'

From Tony's cluttered bedside table Beatrice picked up a cigarette box and Mrs George took a cigarette with shaking fingers. Beatrice glanced around. 'The room looks as though a cyclone had struck it,' she remarked. 'Tony is really the most untidy girl.'

The two women strolled up the stairs.

CHAPTER FIVE

Harland was standing at the top of the stairs when Beatrice and Mrs George came up. Beatrice looked puzzled; the Streamlined Job was flushed and uneasy. As she caught Harland's eye her expression changed and a mechanically bright smile flashed on and off like a neon light. She drifted away into the crowd and Beatrice gave the party a swift, appraising look.

'It's picking up,' she said in relief. 'Carey was anxious to have it a success because he's going to climax it by announcing the engagement of his sister Jennie to Miles Aldrich.'

'No less,' commented Harland.

'No less,' Beatrice agreed, with a shadow of a smile. 'So far, the pleasure is all Jennie's.'

'You surprise me. I should have thought an Aldrich would adorn any family. Or doesn't Carey share his brother-in-law-elect's taste for good works?'

'I'll give you a chance to judge for yourself.' Beatrice looked across the room at an attractive man in his middle thirties who was talking to a woman with beetling brows and a formidable chin. One knew at once that she was a Very Important Person, Harland decided. Otherwise she could never have adopted that grenadier tone or worn those superbly dowdy clothes. They were so dated that they took on personality.

The man turned at once and met Beatrice's eyes, excused himself and started toward her. How those two catch each other's signals, Harland thought. He watched Carey move easily through the crowd. A little obvious, perhaps, for a woman of Beatrice's subtle mind, but his charm was unmistakable. At least, Harland corrected his first impression as Carey approached, there were still signs of charm. At the moment, Carey Walker was somewhat the worse for wear from the number of cocktails he had been drinking.

'John,' Beatrice said, 'this is my partner, Carey Walker. John Harland, Carey. An old friend and—' she gave Harland a half-amused, half-challenging look—'a future client.'

'We hope,' Carey said enthusiastically. His hand shake was firm and his smile sincere. 'I know your book, *Man's Worst Enemy*, and I disliked it very much.'

'Carey!' Beatrice protested.

'Of course I disliked it,' he insisted. 'I prefer to think someone else is to blame for my shortcomings and after reading your book I can't do it any more.'

Harland laughed and Beatrice said in a low tone, her eyes on the Streamlined Job who had become stranded, 'Be nice to Mrs George, will you? She's been rather neglected.' She explained to Harland, 'The Hazel George

Charm School, you know.'

Harland saw the girl with the bruised face approaching and watched her take Carey's arm with a possessive gesture.

'Carey, darling,' she began.

'Tony,' Carey said, 'this is Mr Harland, an old friend of Beatrice's.'

Tony looked at Harland's white hair. 'What fun for you,' she said to Beatrice, 'to meet a friend of your youth.'

'Fun for me,' Harland said quickly, 'to rediscover the most charming woman I know.'

'What kind things you say,' Tony told him. 'But you look kind.' She held out her soft little hand. 'I wondered who you were. I suppose everyone tells you how distinguished you look.' She patted the bruise under her eye with her handkerchief. 'Speaking of looks, I've been going from guest to guest explaining that Carey doesn't beat me. But he'd better take good care of me, hadn't he? If anything happened now it would seem mighty suspicious.'

Harland watched the vein in Carey's temple begin to swell and throb.

'Carey,' Beatrice said quickly, 'you must go amuse Mrs George.' She turned to Harland. 'I am going to present you to Mrs Harrison Ives.'

'Don't wear yourself out,' Tony told her sweetly. 'You look after the clients. I'll deal with the social part of it.'

Beatrice caught her lip between her teeth and

made no reply. She led Harland across the room to the grenadier and performed the introductions. Mrs Harrison Ives inclined her head. Her color was bad and she seemed to be breathing with difficulty.

'Let me get you a chair,' Harland suggested. 'It has been a particularly trying summer, I think, or perhaps—' the smile warmed his eyes before it reached his lips—'I am out of my element at parties.'

Beatrice laughed. 'John, you fraud!' She explained to Mrs Harrison Ives, 'This is *the* John Harland, you know.'

The dowager's expression changed. It was not only more gracious, it was relieved. Why, Harland thought, the woman is frightened!

'Sit down and talk to me,' she commanded.

Beatrice smiled at Harland. 'I see that it is safe to leave you. You are rapidly becoming my pet lion.'

'I'll roar you as gently as any sucking dove,' Harland said obligingly. 'I'll roar you as 'twere a nightingale.'

'Just be yourself,' she told him, 'and this party will go down in history.' She drifted away to join a stray guest who was trying to conceal his isolation by looking fixedly at a modernistic picture.

'Miss Comstock is so competent,' Mrs Harrison Ives remarked.

'I don't know her in her professional capacity,' Harland admitted. 'When she was a

55

little girl, we were neighbors. We have just rediscovered each other.'

'You are a stranger here too.' Mrs Harrison Ives spoke like a woman whose limousine had broken down and who found herself for the first time in a subway crowd. 'Such extraordinary people. Where can they come from? There's not a soul one knows.' She looked at Harland as though they were fellow sufferers. 'It would be interesting to know the opinion of a trained psychologist on all these people.'

'Snap judgments,' Harland said, 'are a bit out of my line.'

'But how,' she persisted, 'do you judge people?'

'I put them together like a jigsaw puzzle,' he admitted. 'A piece here and a piece there. If I have opportunity enough, I eventually get a portrait. The danger lies in trying to guess at the finished likeness from the scattered pieces.'

'I don't quite see what you mean.'

'A little blue piece,' he said idly, his eyes following Tony who was standing beside Carey, laughing up at him from her bruised face. 'I try and fit it into the sky because I am misled by the color. Then I discover that it is part of a woman's skirt and its meaning changes.'

'I have no patience with analogies,' Mrs Harrison Ives said.

Harland was buttonholed by someone who

recognized him and by the time he escaped, Beatrice was coming toward him with three people: a woman with a bright, mischievous smile; a tall, awkward girl who resembled Carey; and a prim-looking man.

'Carey's mother, his sister Jennie, and Mr Aldrich. This is John Harland.'

Harland shook hands with Miles, who said earnestly, 'Harland—Harland, *Man's Worst Enemy!*'

Jennie, who could not learn how to modulate her voice, bleated with laughter. 'Miles!'

'I hadn't thought of it that way,' Harland admitted in amusement.

'Your book is most impressive,' Miles assured him. 'You are quite right—we are our own worst enemies. I have ordered copies sent to all our heads of departments. Food for thought.'

'I hope,' Harland said, 'they will find it digestible.'

'You may be sure that it will be read,' Miles said without emphasis, and Harland revised his first impression. The man was far from negative.

He caught Margaret Walker's dancing eyes and thought, what fun she is. And observing the faint blush that crept over her cheekbones, he knew that she was ashamed of laughing at her daughter's fiancé and he added, how nice she is.

He cut her out neatly and led her to the

terrace.

'I haven't spoken to my daughter-in-law yet,' she protested.

'She is playing hostess,' Harland told her firmly. 'There is plenty of time.'

Margaret looked up at the narrow face with its deep-set eyes. 'From the way Miles spoke,' she began, desperately, 'it's obvious that you must be one of those brilliant men. But if you think I can talk about your book, you're terribly mistaken. I'm not at all clever and I never read.'

'I don't want you to talk about my book,' he assured her. 'But it's more than likely I'll want you to talk about me.'

'Perhaps,' she said, a glint of mischief in her eyes, 'that wouldn't be too difficult.'

Harland groaned. 'We're being invaded.'

Tony came out on the terrace, a cocktail glass in her hand. 'Oh, hello, mother.'

'Heavens, Tony,' Margaret exclaimed, 'what happened to you?'

'A burglar,' Tony said.

'How awful!'

'That's why I couldn't come last night to meet Jennie's fiancé. I was sick about it because I'm longing to meet him. But I was in bed, simply swathed in poultices.'

'But how could a burglar get in? I thought this place was as safe as a bank.' Tony shrugged her shoulders. 'And why on earth did he beat you like that?'

'He took my jewelry,' Tony said. 'I was probably a fool but I tried to stop him and he struck me.'

'Did you call the police?'

'Of course. But I couldn't identify the man— the room was dark.'

Struck you? Harland thought. Someone beat hell out of you, my girl. And how did you know he had taken your jewelry if the room was dark? The story was so palpably false that he studied her with the first real interest he had felt. Carey's second wife was a liar. Certainly, she was a curious choice for a man who had had discrimination enough to be attracted by Beatrice. But at least there was no doubt as to where her attractions lay.

Tony's eyes moved from Margaret to Harland. 'Didn't Carey tell you about it last night?'

'Not a word,' Margaret said.

'Odd.' A smile flickered at the corner of Tony's lips. She turned as Carey came out on the terrace with Miles Aldrich, and stood waiting.

It was curious, Harland thought; they were all waiting for something crucial to happen. Margaret Walker was standing motionless as though braced for a blow.

'Tony,' Carey said, 'this is Jennie's fiancé, Miles Aldrich. My wife, Miles.'

Tony's eyes widened. 'Oh,' she said softly, 'I didn't know you'd be like this.'

59

Harland watched a blush creep over Miles's face.

'I'm going to call you Miles because you are going to be my brother. And I want to hear how you fell in love with Jennie. I've always thought she was madly attractive.'

Across the room Jennie let out a hoot of laughter. Miles glanced from Jennie to Tony who was smiling up at him.

'Let's go around to the side where the voices don't sound so loud,' she said softly, 'and I'll show you my flowers. Do you like flowers, Miles?' As they went out of sight her voice drifted back to them, high and sweet. 'I never dreamed you were like this. From Jennie's description, I mean. The only impression I got was money. Why didn't she tell me how attractive you are?'

Carey turned on his heel and went inside. Margaret looked past him into the living-room and her expression became one of consternation.

'This,' she told Harland, 'is really the last straw.'

'Now what?'

'Jennie's admirer, David Morehouse, has crashed the party—that big, red-headed man who is talking to her. Oh, dear, I hope Miles and Tony come back soon. David dislikes Miles enough as it is.'

*　　*　　*

60

Carey came out on the terrace and closed the door behind him. 'Where's Miles?' he asked. 'People are beginning to leave and I've got to announce the engagement.'

'They haven't come back yet,' Margaret said. 'He's with Tony.'

'All this time? It's almost an hour.'

As he started around the side of the terrace, Margaret said, 'Please, Carey, don't.'

'I'm going to bring them back, dead or alive,' Carey said.

'Let Mr Harland go,' Margaret suggested. 'You've had too much to drink. For Jennie's sake, don't quarrel with Miles.'

Before Carey could reply, the door to the living-room opened and Jennie came out with David Morehouse beside her, and Beatrice close behind. Mrs George managed to slip outside before David closed the door. She tried to cover her dogged determination to interrupt a family conference by an air of false gaiety. 'I didn't like to go,' she said, 'without saying good-by to my hostess.'

'Yes, what's happened to Tony?' Beatrice asked. 'Everyone is looking for her.'

And at that moment Tony came strolling around the corner of the terrace with Miles at her side. As he caught sight of the little group of people he braced himself and approached with an air of detached politeness. The man's ignorance of the telltale mark of lipstick on his face, should, Harland thought, have been

61

laughable but there was nothing funny in the situation. The tension was almost unbearable.

In the silence that followed their appearance, Tony glanced coolly from face to face, from Margaret's stricken eyes to Carey's bloodshot ones, from Beatrice's shocked disbelief to David Morehouse's sudden fury, from Harland's penetrating glance to Mrs George's amused one. Last of all she looked at Jennie, whose face had gone first white and then red.

It was David who got in his word first. 'So that's what you've been up to,' he began.

'Oh, no, David,' Margaret half whispered in distress.

The steady succession of cocktails had stripped Carey of control. 'You little tramp,' he said savagely to Tony, 'I warned you what I'd do if you ever got out of line again.'

'Why, Carey.' The words were a soft, bewildered protest. Tony, looking small and helpless, shrank back, one hand covering the swelling under her eye. 'Why, Carey,' she whimpered, 'just because Miles and I—' She looked up at Miles and saw the mark of the lipstick.

And she laughed.

That tears it, Harland thought, and he waited for the explosion.

'Our guests are waiting,' Beatrice said. 'We can't leave them.'

Carey turned to Miles. He was swaying

slightly. 'I was looking for you,' he said, the words blurred. 'It's customary to have a couple on hand when you announce their engagement. Or hadn't you heard?'

'Really,' Miles expostulated in his prim voice. 'Really, Carey, I—'

'You'd better take that lipstick off first,' Carey said. 'Anyone can see it's not the shade Jennie is wearing.'

'Wait a minute,' Jennie said. 'Wait, Carey! It isn't fair not to give Miles a chance to explain. I know Miles. He—'

'Are you going to accept this?' David demanded.

Miles dabbed at his face with his handkerchief. 'Really,' he began again. 'This is quite unnecessary. And before strangers too. The least you could do, Carey, would be to keep it in the family.'

'That seems to be your idea,' Carey retorted.

'Miles,' Tony said, giving his arm a little pat, 'tell Jennie like a nice boy that you still love her.'

'I don't need any help from you, Tony,' Jennie said. 'Wasn't it enough to break up Carey's marriage? Do you have to take Miles too?'

'Jennie!' Miles expostulated. 'This is absurd. You are being most unfair—most ungenerous—to Tony. She's only trying—'

Jennie looked as though she had been struck. 'You're defending her against me,' she said as though she did not believe it. 'You've been making love to her just when our engagement was to be announced.' Tears ran down her cheeks, she was sniffling. Poor Jennie, Harland thought. Even her grief is unbecoming.

Jennie turned on Tony. 'You're vulgar and common and bad.' Her voice rose hysterically. 'I wish you were dead! I thought Miles was different. And you've made him as cheap as you are.'

David took her arm. 'Come on,' he said, 'we're getting out of here, Jennie.' He pulled her toward the door and looked back at Miles. 'Get ready to duck,' he said, 'because the next time we meet I'm going to beat the living tar out of you.'

The outside door slammed behind them.

'Well,' said Mrs George. Her eyes were bright with excitement. 'Well!' When no one spoke she turned with practiced grace and bowed herself off the terrace.

Beatrice's slim hands swept out in a despairing gesture. Then she lifted her chin and went smiling into the living-room where the guests waited.

CHAPTER SIX

The next morning Carey came into the office and stood watching Beatrice who was typing busily.

'You are limp as a rag, Trix. Why don't you knock off for a few days? This heat wave is getting you down.'

'I'm all right,' she said, trying to give her voice its usual incisiveness. 'And someone has to be here while Miss Campbell is on vacation.'

Carey leaned against her desk. It was extraordinary, she thought, how strong the family resemblance was between him and Jennie, and yet Jennie had no trace of his charm. She was just big, breezy Jennie. Or was she? I've known her for years and never suspected she had Carey's temper. Beatrice wondered whether she dared mention Jennie and the scene that had terminated yesterday's party and decided against it. Better wait for Carey to broach the subject. Usually he was the very model of a successful young executive but today his features were bloated, and there were lines under his bloodshot eyes. He must have got very drunk after John Harland had taken her away the night before. He did not refer to that either. The change in him frightened her. What was Tony doing to him? It's ridiculous, she thought, that we can't talk to each other any more.

'Let the typing go,' he said, 'until Campbell gets back. I could hear you pounding away even with the door of my room shut.'

'Sorry I disturbed you.' Beatrice began a brisk rata-tat-tat.

'You know I didn't mean that,' he said in exasperation. 'You didn't use to twist everything I say like this. All I meant was that there's no need to make a slave of yourself.' She pulled back the carriage with a jerk. Carey's hand swooped over hers so that she could not type. 'We're still friends, aren't we?'

She looked up at him with the warm smile that lighted her face and made her so much younger.

'Your eyes are tired,' he said, his voice uncertain as though he were groping for something. 'You mustn't strain them. They are still the loveliest eyes in the world.'

Beatrice snatched her hand away and began to pound the typewriter.

'Sorry I was out of order,' he said with a hurt tone in his voice.

'Stop acting, Carey! When a thing is done it's done. Can't you get that into your head? And don't interrupt me. I've got to finish these notes on the Hazel George campaign. You'll need them when you see her this morning. Don't forget you have an eleven o'clock appointment. There isn't much time.'

She leaned back in her chair. 'There's

something queer about that woman,' she said, and she described finding Mrs George searching the drawers of Tony's dressing table. 'What do you suppose she was up to?'

'God knows. I wondered why she insisted on hanging on to the bitter end.'

'Obviously she wanted to talk to Tony. But why?'

'At least,' Carey said, 'we provided her with plenty of entertainment.'

A radio blared and Beatrice pushed back her damp hair with a nervous gesture.

'Damn it,' Carey said, 'I've asked Tony a dozen times to keep that thing tuned low. She sits in her bath for a solid hour with the radio raising such a rumpus it can be heard a block away. I put out a lot of money for this place and she turns it into Coney Island.'

'We'd better get to work.' Beatrice's voice was clipped and businesslike. 'It's ten-fifteen. I think the best angles for Mrs George—'

But Carey was in one of his unpredictable moods. As a rule, he was intent and absorbed when it came to planning a campaign. His enthusiasm carried everything before it. He refused to acknowledge that there could be any unsurmountable obstacles. But this morning he was indifferent.

'Skip it,' he said. 'I've got a head the size of a house and a whole army of carpenters hammering on it. I'm in no mood for charm. How the hell does she teach charm anyhow?'

67

'Well,' Beatrice considered, 'what she really does is reduce them—sweating or whacking or exercising or steaming off weight. Women who go to her are mostly over forty. Then she shows them how to stand and sit and walk—'

'Haven't they learned how to do that by the time they're forty?'

It was good to be laughing together with the companionship they had had for six years, but Beatrice came back to business.

'So the angle we've got to play up is the middle-aged charmers, Ninon de Lenclos and all that. Now—'

Carey was always impressed by her staccato manner when she was selling an idea, but now he interrupted. 'All right. I get it.' Someone was singing on the radio, a woman with a nasal voice and powerful lungs, lugubriously calling back her lost love. 'God! This place is a boiler factory.' He scooped up the contracts and Beatrice's notes and slammed out of the office.

Beatrice leaned forward, elbows on her typewriter, head gripped in her hands. Everyone's temper was short in a heat wave. It did things to people. There was something in that phrase, 'Crazy with the heat.' They were all on edge. Even Jennie. She turned in her chair so that she sat looking down on the river and the fat tugboats and the traffic streaming along the highway.

'Yes, Freda?' she said without turning as the maid appeared in the doorway.

'Mr Aldrich to see Mr Walker.'

'Mr Walker has gone out on a conference with a client. I don't know when he'll be back.' Beatrice hesitated. 'Let Mr Aldrich know I am here if I can help.'

'Yes, madam—Miss Comstock.' Freda, who had been housemaid before Beatrice's divorce, was flustered at her blunder and hurried away.

There were a series of squawks as the radio was switched from station to station and Beatrice set her teeth. She glanced expectantly toward the door but Miles did not come. Had he called to explain his behavior to Carey? Had he seen Jennie and were things all right with them? Or had the belligerent reporter seized the golden hour and caught Jennie on the rebound?

Beatrice turned to the window, unable to fix her mind on her work. Waiting. She heard someone come down the stairs and go past the office. At this hour it was probably Freda. That radio was really impossible. Tony had a soap opera on now, the voices high and shrill. No, that was Tony's own voice. If she had begun to abuse the servants, it was really time to interfere. Beatrice half rose and then hesitated. In a few moments she heard footsteps on the stairs again, going up, stumbling.

For a long time she looked unseeingly out of the window. Then she felt a sudden urge to turn her head, as though someone were looking at her. She stood still, listening. No one. And yet instinct told her that she was not alone.

She turned abruptly. The office was empty and so was the reception room. There was no one on the stairs, but somewhere above there were muffled footsteps. Freda, of course. But the uneasy feeling would not go.

She took a long breath and then went down the hall to Tony's bedroom. The door was ajar and Tony was still in her bath. There was no answer to the light rap.

'Tony,' Beatrice called, and more sharply, 'Tony!' After a moment's hesitation she went in. The door to the bathroom stood wide open.

*　　　*　　　*

Beatrice held on to the washbowl with both hands. She had stopped being sick but she was shaking so violently she could not stand without support. You've got to think, she told herself.

She took a step and realized that she had been standing in a pool of water. It must have splashed over the edge of the tub. She hadn't noticed. She was careful not to glance toward the tub. Her legs were rubbery but she turned and stumbled into Tony's exquisite, untidy room and sank down on the side of the bed. She fought against the black wave that crept over her eyes, over her mind, and set her finger firmly on the bell. She did not open her eyes until the maid came in with the breakfast tray.

'Freda,' she framed the words with difficulty, 'call Dr Robinson, will you?'

'Are you sick, Miss Comstock?' the maid asked in concern, setting down the breakfast tray with a faint, musical tinkle of silver.

'No,' Beatrice wet her lips. 'It's Mrs Walker. She's—had an accident.'

Freda looked in the bathroom, took a step forward and screamed, the sounds tearing from her throat, and then choked off as though a hand had clamped over her mouth.

'What's all the rumpus?' Carey asked irritably from the doorway. He looked from the maid to Beatrice's gray, horror-struck face.

'Carey! I thought you were out.'

'What's wrong?'

She gestured with one shaking hand toward the bathroom door. Carey went inside. She saw him standing beside the tub. He did not move or touch anything. He simply looked. Beatrice shut her eyes but she could not shut out the picture that Carey was seeing—Tony's face distorted by its hideous grimace, her twisted hand, her—Beatrice fought down the mounting nausea.

At length Carey came back and closed the bathroom door behind him. He did not look at her. Pulling out a handkerchief, he wiped his forehead.

'What do I give Freda?' he asked in a low voice as though afraid of disturbing the girl in the bathtub. 'I think she's fainted.'

'Water,' Beatrice said, and then drew in her breath with a hiss. 'I mean—some aromatic spirits of ammonia, if there is any.'

'There's a bottle upstairs,' Carey said, still in his hushed voice, and he went out, walking on tiptoe.

Beatrice reached for the telephone with a steady hand and dialed a number.

'Dr Robinson? ... This is Beatrice Comstock. Please come to Mr Walker's penthouse at once. There has been a horrible accident... No, Mrs Walker... She's dead... I think she was electrocuted ... The radio...'

Freda opened her eyes, heard Beatrice's words and began to cry, loud, strangling sobs.

'Is that necessary, doctor?' Beatrice asked. 'Of course ... Yes, I understand. In that case, I'll attend to it.'

Carey came back into the room. He's had a drink, Beatrice thought dully. He held a glass to Freda's lips.

'Down with it,' he said. 'It's good for you.' He steadied the glass and the maid drank obediently. He patted her shoulder. 'Try to pull yourself together. We're going to need you today.'

Even now, even with that contorted body in the bathtub with the rictus on its face, his tone had that engaging quality that made a woman's heart melt. Freda wiped her face with the handkerchief he had whipped out of his breast pocket. She even managed an uncertain smile.

'I'm all right.' The tears still welled up in her eyes but her voice was steady. 'What shall I do? Shouldn't we take it—her—out of the tub?'

'We have to leave things as they are,' Beatrice said. 'And it doesn't matter to her now, Freda.' She glanced at Carey. 'How do you get a policeman?'

He stood motionless for a moment, as though his breath had been cut off. 'Policeman?'

'Dr Robinson said we would have to report to the police. They have to be told about accidental deaths.'

'Oh, well—I guess you just ask for one.'

Beatrice called the police and made her report. Then she put down the telephone and rested her head on her outstretched arms.

Freda got up. She was a Swede, big, rawboned, her wheat-colored hair wound in thick braids around her head, pale blue eyes that were cowlike in her disciplined face.

'What shall I do first?' she asked.

'That's the girl,' Carey encouraged her. 'You've always been a tower of strength, Freda. I'm depending on you. Be ready to let these people in.' His hand rested on her shoulder for a moment and then the maid went out of the room quietly, without a backward glance.

Carey turned to Beatrice. 'Let's get out—go

upstairs. We can't do any good here.'

'Just a minute.' She dialed John Harland's number.

When she had put back the telephone Carey asked, 'Why did you send for him?'

'Because.' Beatrice got groggily to her feet and Carey half led, half supported her up the stairs and onto the terrace. She stretched out in a deck chair, eyes closed against the light, the lines that made parentheses at the corners of her mouth etched deep. The flesh seemed to have shrunk on her cheeks. This is how she will look when she is an old woman, Carey thought.

The chime of the doorbell rang and Beatrice, with an effort of will, became brisk and competent. 'Don't say too much, Carey. We've got to consider all the angles.'

She broke off as Freda came out on the terrace followed by the police.

CHAPTER SEVEN

Harland, his white hair accentuated by an immaculate white suit, his narrow face troubled, followed the solemn butler out onto the terrace where Beatrice lay in the deck chair.

'It was good of you to come,' she said. 'There was no excuse for my calling you. But the thing was such a shock and I didn't want to be alone.

I needed a friend. It was horribly selfish.'

'The nicest compliment you could have paid,' he assured her. 'Do you feel like telling me what happened or would you rather not talk about it?'

'It's Tony,' she said. 'She's dead.'

'Yes, I understood that. How did it happen?'

'She was taking a bath and there was a radio at the side of the tub. It fell in and she was—electrocuted.' Beatrice gathered together her scattered forces and added, 'I found her.'

Harland gave a shocked exclamation, but after a glance at her haggard face he asked no questions. She sat up with a quick, decisive gesture.

'I simply can't go to pieces,' she said. 'There is so much to be done.'

'Let me be useful.'

'You are, John. Just by being here.' And it was true, she thought. Harland's presence brought with it a kind of reassurance. Nothing surprised him, nothing seemed impossible for him. Even this horror. Somehow John would be able to deal with it. She went on, 'Carey is down there now with the police. Dr Robinson said we had to call them. They've been here a long time. And they've sent for more men and photographers. Why should that be necessary?'

'They have to be sure, you know.'

'Sure of what?' she asked sharply. Her voice broke. 'Oh, John, I told you she'd make trouble, one way or another.'

'Steady,' he said.

The butler appeared in the doorway and caught Beatrice's eye. With a murmured excuse she went inside. Harland waited until she was out of earshot and then he said, without raising his voice, 'It must be hot around there, Mr Aldrich. Why don't you join me here in the shade?' He did not turn his head as Miles came around the corner of the terrace and sat down beside him.

It struck Harland that Miles Aldrich should be growing accustomed to being found in anomalous positions but now, as the afternoon before, he seemed to feel that he could deal with the situation by ignoring it.

'How did you guess I was there?'

Harland smiled. 'I never guess. I heard you. New York is a trying climate for asthma.'

Miles polished his eyeglasses with an immaculate handkerchief and patted his forehead lightly. 'One hardly knows what is the best thing to do at a time like this. Whether to come forward and offer one's services and risk being a nuisance, or to stay in the background.'

He was holding himself under rigid control but, to Harland's searching eyes, he seemed more upset than the occasion warranted. Interesting as he had appeared to find Tony the day before, it had, after all, been his first meeting with her. One is not usually shattered by the death—even so shocking a death—of a

76

comparative stranger.

Harland's silence did not have its usual tranquilizing effect. Miles fidgeted in his chair.

'The police in the house! The story in the papers! And probably no effort to minimize the publicity. It will involve us all. A man in Carey's position wouldn't think of that.'

'Oh, come,' Harland expostulated, 'you can hardly believe that Mr Walker would capitalize on the death of his own wife.'

'Of course not.' There was no conviction in Miles's tone. 'Though he's not a type for whom I have any particular sympathy. Not at all like his sister.' He gritted his teeth.

I've often read of people doing that but I've never seen it done before, Harland thought.

There were women's voices in the living-room and Margaret Walker came out on the terrace, her piquant face drawn with anxiety. The two men rose to greet her. She nodded to Harland and held out her hand to Miles.

'I didn't know Carey had sent for you,' she said. 'I was too shocked to think of it when he called. But I'm so glad you are here. It will help Jennie when she comes.'

Something in her voice, her unquestioning trust, the reliance which she put on him, brought a flush to Miles's cheeks and he pressed her hand without speaking.

'I left the shop as soon as Carey telephoned,' Margaret went on quickly, 'but I couldn't reach Jennie. She wasn't home. I told the girls to keep calling until they got her and to send her here, but not to let her know—not over the telephone. Poor Tony! What a frightful thing. So young and so happy and so much to live for.'

Nervousness made her chatter as though she could not stop. Now she sank down in the chair Harland pulled up for her.

'Where's Carey?'

'Downstairs with the police,' Harland told her.

But Carey was coming out on the terrace, followed by a man in plain clothes whom he introduced as Lieutenant Mattheson and a uniformed policeman named Sergeant Greer. Behind them came Beatrice and at a word from her the butler brought out more chairs. Beatrice leaned against the railing, her eyes watchful.

Margaret went to Carey and put her arms around him without a word. For a moment he held her and then released her.

'How did it happen?' she asked.

'She was electrocuted.' Carey's face and voice were rigidly controlled. 'The radio fell into the tub.'

Mattheson looked around slowly, taking his time, missing nothing. He recognized Miles Aldrich but the recognition did not alter his manner. When he spoke, he did so without any particular emphasis, his tone so matter of fact that it was a moment before they felt the full impact of his remark.

'We have all been trying to push the radio and it won't budge. It fitted into grooves in that ledge beside the tub. The only way it could be moved would be by lifting it.'

'But that,' Margaret cried out, 'would be deliberate—'

The word murder was unspoken but it crashed over the terrace like thunder. Murder.

'That's right,' the lieutenant said flatly.

Beatrice came forward with the proud carriage so many people mistook for hauteur. 'It could not possibly be murder,' she said crisply. 'I was in the office all morning with the door open on account of the heat. There was no one downstairs at all. Mr Walker had gone out for an appointment, a conference with a client. No one could have come down the stairs without my knowing it. I'd be willing to take my oath on that.'

The lieutenant studied her for a moment. 'The office is behind that white and crimson room,' he said, consulting a rough sketch scrawled on his notebook.

'Yes, but the door was open.'

'And you never took your eyes off the door?'

Beatrice was silent.

'Would you take your oath on that?' the lieutenant persisted.

'No,' she admitted reluctantly. 'But on those marble stairs you can hear footsteps distinctly. I heard Freda when she came down. I'm sure I would have heard anyone else.'

'Freda?'

'The housemaid.'

The lieutenant smiled. 'You see, Miss—'

'Comstock.'

'You see, Miss Comstock. First you are ready to take your oath there was nobody. Now you remember the maid.'

'I hadn't forgotten her,' Beatrice said impatiently. 'Freda has a right to be downstairs.'

'Did you see her?'

'No. I didn't turn around. I just knew it was Freda.'

'You expected it to be.' At Mattheson's request the sergeant lumbered out and returned with the maid.

'What's your name?' Mattheson asked her.

She glanced coolly at Carey who said, 'Give him all the help you can, Freda.'

'I'm Freda Peterson, sir. I'm the maid.'

'How long have you worked here?'

'Five years, sir.' Her voice was calm, with no trace of her hysterical outburst. Her eyes were level. She stood, stolid, reliable, and placid.

'Did you go downstairs this morning?' Mattheson asked her.

'Yes, sir.'

'When?'

She thought gravely. 'First, about eight-thirty when I made up Mr Walker's room and dusted the office. Then,' she glanced at Miles

80

for confirmation, 'about ten-thirty, I think, when Mr Aldrich called to see Mr Walker. I went down to tell Miss Comstock and she said Mr Walker was out. The last time was when Miss Comstock rang.'

'When was that?'

'I'm not just sure,' Freda said. 'The kitchen clock had stopped. I thought it was Mrs Walker ringing for breakfast and it was early for her. She didn't usually ring before eleven-thirty.'

'That's not what I mean,' Mattheson said. 'When you went down before, between ten-thirty and eleven.'

Freda shook her head. 'Those were the only times I was downstairs.'

'But I heard you,' Beatrice said.

'Not me. I was out in the kitchen the whole time.'

'You couldn't have been!' Beatrice was angry. 'I heard Mrs Walker speak to you.'

'No, ma'am.'

Mattheson's tone was sharper. 'You heard Mrs Walker speaking to someone?'

Beatrice hesitated, uncertain. 'I thought I did,' she said at length. 'At first it sounded like a soap opera on the radio and then I recognized Tony's voice. Now I'm not sure.' Her eyes widened. 'But someone did go up the stairs *after* I heard the voices. Someone stumbled.'

'Not me,' Freda said again.

'Were you alone in the kitchen?' Mattheson

asked.

Freda shook her head. 'It's like this. Harris—that's the butler—does the marketing. So he was out and there was no one upstairs but Mrs Harris—the cook—and me. After Mr Aldrich called, there was a short circuit in the kitchen.'

'Naturally,' Mattheson said and Freda looked at him, blankly at first and then with shocked understanding. She went on with an effort, 'Mrs Harris was frantic because the whole kitchen is electrified and she was timing a cake. I was there the whole time, trying to fix the fuses, but they kept blowing out—until the bell rang and I thought Mrs Walker had rung for her breakfast tray—only—' her voice threatened to get out of control—'Mrs Walker couldn't ring.'

It was curious that so flat a statement should conjure up the sharp, horrifying reason why Tony could not have rung the bell.

'Then,' Mattheson's voice broke the silence, 'who went downstairs and stumbled when he went back up again?'

There was no answer. Freda stood with her hands hanging relaxed, her face impassive. She would be an excellent witness, Harland thought, and any jury in the land would believe her. And yet she was holding something back.

He smiled at her. 'What's the matter, Freda? Did you leave the front door open?'

'It was cleaning day,' she explained. 'Once a

week I do the outside hall carpet when I vacuum the foyer of the apartment because the service in the house is slack and they don't do it right. I always leave the latch off while I'm outside. But this morning Mr Aldrich called just as I was coming in and I went downstairs to tell Miss Comstock. When I came upstairs I was busy putting away the cleaning things and then the short circuit happened. I just forgot all about the door.'

Mattheson's lower lip was big and rubbery like that of a comedian. He thrust it up over his upper lip while he meditated. 'How long was it open?'

There were tears in Freda's eyes. 'Ten minutes. Maybe more. I noticed it when I started down with Mrs Walker's tray and shut it then.'

Mattheson pulled hard at his lower lip. Then he swung around to Beatrice. 'First it's nobody, then it's somebody, now it's anybody.' He added, 'You found the body, didn't you?'

'Yes.'

'How did you happen to go in? Did you usually call Mrs Walker?'

Beatrice was silent for a moment. 'No, I didn't,' she admitted. 'I felt—uneasy.'

'Why?'

She made a helpless gesture with her slim hands. 'I don't know why. You'll think, after my telling you about footsteps that weren't there, that I imagine things, but I don't. I was really startled. You know how you feel when someone is looking at you? You have to turn around. You don't know why. It was like that. I felt someone was there.'

She communicated a sense of that unseen presence and Margaret Walker shivered.

'And yet,' Mattheson said, 'you were willing to take your oath no one was there.'

'That's why I know no one was. Because I looked. And then I went to Tony's room and called her. When she didn't answer, I went in.'

'Anything to add to that?'

She shook her head.

'You say you were working in the office. I understand you are Mr Walker's partner. Is that right?'

'Yes.' Beatrice drew a long breath. 'I'd better explain. I was Mr Walker's first wife but we decided to get a divorce. We've gone right on being business partners though.' She smiled wryly. 'If you want a murder suspect, I guess you'll have to pick me.'

'My dear,' Margaret interposed, her face puckered with distress, 'don't talk nonsense.' She looked anxiously at the lieutenant. 'You must not take her seriously,' she said. 'Beatrice and my son are a wonderful team but they just don't like being married.' A smile that was almost conspiratorial hovered on her lips and the lieutenant smiled back. In no time at all, Harland thought in amusement, he'll be

84

dropping around to tell her all his troubles. None the less, he watched Mattheson. The lieutenant's manner was that of a poker player who had an ace in a hole.

'It has to be accident,' Carey said heavily. 'I don't know how the radio slipped but it must have. Tony is—she was careless about things. She wouldn't have noticed if it wasn't set in the notches. Maybe Freda moved it when she cleaned. Freda,' and he managed a stiff smile, 'is a demon cleaner-upper.'

Loyalty has its limits and Freda came of hard-headed and clear-sighted stock.

'I always wiped the radio off but I have never moved it. I'll swear to that.'

'Well, then,' Carey said impatiently, 'perhaps Tony did it herself. She wouldn't know it was dangerous.' He looked around at the still faces, his own gray. 'It's got to be that way. No one would kill her. She was just a kid and a stranger in New York. There was no one—'

'Any family?'

The question took Carey by surprise. 'None she ever mentioned. Her parents died when she was just a baby.'

'Full name?'

'Antonia Smith.'

'Where did she live before she came here?'

'Chicago.' Carey anticipated the next question. 'I don't know the address. The poor kid was having a hard time of it and I expect

85

she lived in some sort of cheap boarding house or furnished room.'

'Any enemies?'

'Of course not.'

'Do you know any of her friends?'

'She didn't know a soul in New York except the people she met through me. She hadn't been happy and she didn't like to talk about the past so we didn't discuss it.'

'All you know,' the detective said stolidly, 'is Antonia Smith, Chicago. Is that right?'

'If I was satisfied,' Carey said, 'that's all that matters, isn't it? When you're in love, you don't think of all those things. But there is no mystery about Tony. She didn't have any enemies. Everyone liked her.'

'Then how,' Mattheson asked, turning up his ace, 'did she get those bruises? Someone gave her a terrible beating. And don't tell me you were so much in love with her that you didn't notice them!'

CHAPTER EIGHT

The eruption of Jennie onto the terrace at that point averted an explosion. She was wearing an unbecoming dress of royal blue and her attempt to acquire the New Look gave her an air of having rummaged through an old trunk for her clothes.

'What goes on?' she demanded. 'Why did you send for me, Mom?'

There was a sound of footsteps on the stairs, the slow tread of men carrying a heavy burden. Jennie glanced into the living-room. The high color faded from her face. 'What—who is it?' she asked in a whisper.

Miles put his arm around her. 'There has been an accident, darling,' he said tenderly. 'Mrs Walker—'

'Tony!' Unconsciously she stiffened, drew away from him. 'What's happened?'

He told her as gently as he could, eased her into a chair and stationed himself beside it. Margaret reached for her daughter's hand and clasped it in her own. They seemed oddly protective.

'This is my daughter Jennie,' Margaret said. 'Lieutenant Mattheson, dear.'

'Miss Walker is my fiancée,' Miles informed Mattheson.

And if you think that will make the police lay off, Harland thought, you are sadly mistaken. For while the detective was obviously not going to bring the Aldrich wrath crashing down on his head if he could avoid it, he was neither frightened nor overawed. If he could not solve his case without clashing with the millionaire, then the clash would occur. Harland felt considerable respect for the police officer who was doing his job without bullying but without favor.

87

Mattheson, who had got to his feet when Jennie appeared, waited until she was seated.

'What goes on?' she demanded. 'Why did you send for me, Mom?'

'We are investigating Mrs Walker's death,' he said abruptly. 'Did your sister-in-law have any enemies, so far as you know?'

'Enemies!' Jennie was dumbfounded. 'Was there something—wrong about Tony's death? I mean—'

'That's what we are trying to determine. Did she have any reason for killing herself?'

'Heavens, no! Tony always got everything she wanted!' Resentment and dislike were so apparent in Jennie's bitter words that the lieutenant's attention sharpened.

'When did you see her last?'

Beatrice intervened swiftly. 'At the cocktail party yesterday.'

Mattheson's expression was one of cold fury but Jennie had been warned. There was nothing to do about it—for the moment, at any rate.

'Did Mrs Walker have any bruises yesterday?'

'Oh, yes,' Jennie said readily. 'She looked awful. Everyone was talking about it.'

'Did she explain how she got them?'

'Of course. The burglar.'

'What's this?' Mattheson demanded. 'Why hasn't anyone told me?'

It was Carey who explained. 'Sorry,

Lieutenant,' he said. 'I simply hadn't thought of it. My wife's—horrible death drove it completely out of my mind. The burglary happened night before last.' He explained that he and Beatrice had kept an appointment with a client and that on his return home he had found a police prowl car at the door.

'Seems we'd had a burglar while I was out; he took some of my wife's jewelry and when she tried to stop him he got rough and knocked her around. As soon as he had gone she called the police and reported it.'

'This burglar inflicted those marks on her?' Mattheson said alertly.

Carey nodded.

'Did she give the police a description?'

'No,' Carey said, 'she couldn't describe him.' He was, Harland thought, too careful. He volunteered nothing.

'What did he get away with?'

'My wife found only one thing missing,' Carey said. 'An emerald necklace.'

'Valuable?'

Carey wet his lips. 'Twenty thousand dollars.'

That brought the break for which Mattheson was waiting. 'A necklace worth twenty thousand dollars,' Margaret scoffed. 'Where on earth could Tony have got anything like that?'

Mattheson turned abruptly to Jennie. 'Did you ever see such a necklace, Miss Walker?'

Before she could answer, voices were raised in argument, there were sounds of a scuffle, and David Morehouse, his red hair ruffled, pushed aside the butler and stood in the doorway.

'Jennie,' he said quickly, 'you don't have to answer any questions without seeing a lawyer.'

'Harris,' Beatrice said, and the butler appeared with an outraged glare for David, 'serve a buffet lunch on the terrace, will you? We've got to eat. And, Carey, you might mix some drinks. We all need them.'

'Suppose,' Carey said disagreeably, 'you let me be host in my own apartment.'

Beatrice looked at him in disbelief and then her cheeks flamed. 'I'm sorry,' she said. 'I—' She turned to Mattheson, stripped of her self-possession. 'If you don't need me any longer—'

'Not now,' he said. 'Give Sergeant Greer your address and don't leave town.'

Harland supplied his name and address, said good-by, grasped David by the arm and propelled him toward the door. They caught up with Beatrice as she was stepping into the elevator.

'You are both,' Harland said, 'going to lunch with me.'

'I've got to get back there,' David protested, 'and look out for Jennie.'

Harland's grip tightened, he gave a quick twist that threw David off balance and propelled him into the elevator.

David looked at Harland's slight frame and asked in a tone of wonder, 'How did you do that?'

'Judo.'

'It's a good trick but I've got to go back. I have a job to do,' the boy insisted.

'We all,' Harland said grimly, 'have a job to do.'

*   *   *

When they reached the street, the hot air struck them like a blow. The sidewalks wavered.

'Where can we go to get out of this heat?' Beatrice asked.

'My house,' Harland said. He hailed a cab, handed her in and waved for David to precede him.

'Don't tell me you've snagged a whole house to yourself, John!'

'A nice one. You're going to like it.'

'How did you do it?' she asked as the taxi turned down Fifth Avenue toward the Washington Arch.

'The house? Friend of mine,' he said vaguely.

'Did you go in shooting?'

He was amused. 'Not quite.'

'Rent free for the season while the owner goes abroad, I suppose,' Beatrice said bitterly.

'Well, no. As a matter of fact, he gave it to me.'

'Gave you a house! Whatever for?'

'My old weakness. Solving puzzles.'

The taxi turned a corner and the driver called, 'What was that number?'

'Stop here.'

A high wall ran along the street and Beatrice looked around curiously and then turned to Harland with a question in her eyes.

He smiled teasingly. 'You'll see.'

'How you love mysteries!'

He pulled out a key, unlocked a door set in the high wall and opened it with a flourish. They walked into a garden at the end of which stood a square, white, three-story house.

The reporter whistled and Beatrice declared, 'I didn't know there was anything like this in New York.'

'Few people do,' Harland acknowledged.

There was a fanlight over the doorway and Beatrice refused to budge until she had had time to admire the details. When he opened the door she cried out in delight. The entrance led directly into a high, two-story living-room lined with books. In the right wall there was a gigantic fireplace, and books extended even above and across the mantel to the ceiling, reached by a small ladder which slid along a rod. In one corner a circular staircase, delicate as a spiderweb, wound steeply up to a balcony on the second-floor level.

'It's a dream room,' Beatrice declared. 'It just suits you, John.'

'Somehow,' he told her, 'I think you mean that as a very nice compliment.'

'Of course I do. You are a very nice person.'

'When you have eaten one of Mrs Larsen's lunches,' he assured her complacently, 'you are going to adore me.'

When his housekeeper had set one of her delectable lunches before them and withdrawn, Harland glanced at his two silent guests and smiled. 'Perhaps,' he said, 'I was a shade peremptory but—'

'I know,' David said. 'You thought I was going to stir things up. But—'

'We'll discuss it after lunch,' Harland said.

'What I want to know,' David demanded, 'is whether Tony Walker was murdered or died accidentally. The news that came over the office ticker didn't say.'

'After lunch,' Harland said firmly. 'Mrs Larsen's cooking is not to be spoiled.'

David capitulated with a grin. 'You sound just the way you did at Dartmouth. "After we have dealt with the fundamentals, gentlemen, we will have time for the trivialities."'

'You know me?' Harland asked in surprise, and Beatrice gave him a glance of amused affection. The fact that he was a celebrity had never dawned on him.

'Sure I know you,' David said. 'You lectured when I was a senior. I recognized you yesterday at the cocktail party. By the way, show me how you got that grip on me, will you?'

93

'Delighted. Beatrice, you aren't eating anything. If you neglect Mrs Larsen's cooking I'll never ask you again.'

David looked up from his plate to say, 'I've thought a lot about those lectures of yours. You talked about humanics, the study of human nature. And you said no one had ever tried to study the whole man. Just bits and pieces, without fitting them together, without getting down to what made them tick. You said each man got hold of one part and thought he had the whole animal: the psychoanalyst, the physician, the neurologist, the anthropologist, the sociologist, the economist, the artist. But they didn't put together their knowledge. Is that still your subject?'

'Still my subject, though I don't devote all my time to writing now. The study of human nature—it takes in a lot of territory. Everything is related to everything else if you can only see its broader aspects. So I find myself going down some queer bypaths.'

'Such as?' David asked alertly.

'Crime, for one thing.'

'So you are the John Harland who found Jean Clark.'

'I'm the one.'

'But why crime?' David persisted.

'It fascinates me,' Harland confessed. 'I've always had a weakness for puzzles. Ask Beatrice—she knows. Combine that with an insatiable curiosity about human behavior and you have me.'

'You must have some swell stories up your sleeve,' David said wistfully. 'If I were still on the paper—'

'I thought you were a reporter,' Beatrice said in surprise.

David was brick red. 'They'd just sent me out to cover a story when news about Tony came over the ticker. I thought—anyhow I decided I'd better hie me up there and see what was cooking. Not that I cared about the job.' He leaned back in his chair with a sigh of repletion. The great book-lined room was dim and cool. He had eaten the major part of a golden, fluffy omelet, flaky muffins dripping with butter, crisp salad from a frosty bowl.

'How do you keep so thin on food like that?' Beatrice commented. 'I'd bulge within a week,' and she stroked a slim hip apprehensively.

She was spectacularly black and white, a sheer, simple black dress and a large white cartwheel tilted at an extreme angle on her dark hair.

Harland looked at her in appreciation. 'You are an attractive woman,' he said, 'but I always expected you would be. Now I have fed you both superlatively and I intend to be paid for it. Together, we are going to sift out what you both know that might have any bearing on Tony Walker's death.'

He had always, Beatrice remembered, had a real interest in people, one that brought him

95

surprising confidences, and that collected small children and old ladies around him like flies around honey. He never found their conversation dull or prosy.

Harland turned to David. 'Of course,' he admitted, 'I practically kidnaped you; I'm not usually so high handed but Lieutenant Mattheson is an astute detective, from what I saw of him, and I thought we'd better think the situation through before there were any—indiscretions.'

David tapped a cigarette on the arm of his chair and made no reply.

'You threw up your job and went charging up to the Walker penthouse,' Harland said, 'because you were afraid when you heard the news about Tony. Afraid that Jennie might be in trouble because of that quarrel she had yesterday. Motive, and all that.'

'Don't put any words into my mouth,' David said quickly. 'Jennie wouldn't have done anything to Tony. But people can get into trouble whether they rate it or not. Jennie's a nice kid.' He kept his tone carefully casual. 'Real. And kind. Too good for old Frozen Face.'

'Aldrich? What have you got against him?' Harland asked idly.

'Plenty,' David said with vigor. 'Even before he cut me out with Jennie I thought he was a skunk.'

'Why?'

'Well, look at his father's record, for one thing.'

'He's not to blame for that,' Harland said reasonably.

'And the way he treated his brother. I'll admit Graham Aldrich was a first-class heel but at least he was human.'

'Did you know him?'

'Everyone who got around to night spots and all that knew Graham. At least by sight. Especially,' David grinned, 'anyone who watched the police blotter. He was always being booked: drunk and disorderly, speeding; they even got him once on a hit-run charge.'

'And what did Aldrich do to him?'

'That's what I would like to know,' David said darkly. 'Graham was at some club about a year ago. He was tight as usual and got in a row. Miles had been nasty about Graham's brawls and all the publicity. He's a glutton for publicity himself but not that kind. Nothing unpleasant. Nothing scandalous.'

'What kind does he like?' Beatrice asked with her first display of interest, and Harland's eyes twinkled with amusement.

'Having the world know when he builds a church or endows a hospital or takes slum kids to his summer camp. He has kissed more babies for the photographers than any politician in the country.'

Beatrice nodded. 'That's the angle I figured. The great humanitarian. I had a honey of a campaign worked out and I am positive we could have sold it to Miles without any trouble,but Carey didn't want any part of it.'

'And what,' Harland asked, 'happened to Graham Aldrich?'

'Well,' David said, 'he got in this brawl. He couldn't have been badly hurt because he went home under his own steam. But the next morning he was found dead on the floor of his bedroom. Broken neck. Then the newspapers dropped it like a hot potato. But there was no real investigation and the doctor who testified got to be a big shot at a hospital Aldrich endowed.'

'In other words,' Harland said, 'if Graham was not injured at the night club, someone broke his neck after he got home.'

David nodded and waited for Harland's comment. When none was forthcoming he prodded, 'Well, what do you think?'

'With no more to go on,' Harland replied mildly, 'I'd reserve judgment. Now let's put our heads together and see what can be done about Tony's death.'

'You think it was murder, don't you?' David asked bluntly.

'The police think so, which is more to the point.'

'And yet,' Beatrice said, 'I don't see how they could prove it.'

'Don't underestimate them.'

'Or why anyone would do it.'

'Oh, motive!' Harland smiled. 'I can think of at least four sound motives without half trying.'

David leaned forward. 'You're going to work on this, aren't you?'

'Yes,' Harland said, 'in my own peculiar way.'

'Am I in it with you, sir?'

'That's what I hoped. I need someone to do leg work. As long as you are temporarily free, how would you like to take a job with me?'

'Doing what?'

'Finding out how Tony Walker died.' His bony fingers beat a restless tattoo on the arm of his chair.

'But we know,' Beatrice intervened, 'how she died.'

'Then let's say—why she died.' He was silent for a moment and they waited while he assembled his thoughts. 'We know that the front door of the duplex was open, which means that anyone in New York could have got in the apartment at the time Tony was killed.'

'It's a big territory,' David commented.

'Not so big. There has to be a powerful motive to make a person take an appalling risk like that. And motive is harder to conceal than a human body. In a sense, motive is the only thing that can't be concealed. We've got to bear in mind the fact that the crime was an impulse.'

'How do you know?' David asked.

'Because no one could have foreseen that the door would be open and unguarded. And no one in his right mind would ring the bell, have a servant admit him, commit a murder, and expect to get away with it.' He glanced at Beatrice. 'What is it,' he asked quickly, 'that you have just remembered?'

'Who called Miles?' she demanded. 'Who told him that Tony was dead? I didn't call anyone but Dr Robinson, the police, and you. Carey made only one call and that was to his mother.'

'It is possible,' Harland suggested, 'that Miles never left the apartment at all. When I arrived, he was out of sight around the corner of the terrace. Positively lurking. He was there while you and I were talking.'

'But Miles Aldrich,' Beatrice began, her face blank with bewilderment. 'Why should he hurt Tony? You saw for yourself what happened yesterday when he met her. I'll never forget how he looked, with that air of outraged innocence and the lipstick on his face. He went overboard. She had that effect on men. You didn't know Tony.'

'Nobody seems to have known Tony. Antonia Smith, Chicago. No family. No friends. No past. A twenty thousand dollar emerald necklace—and a burglar who gives her a beating.'

'Do you think,' Beatrice said slowly, 'that

the burglar was someone she knew?'

'It seems more than likely.'

'But she didn't know any—but—then the whole story about the burglar was wrong. And that necklace—Carey couldn't possibly buy a twenty thousand dollar necklace. I know his bank balance as well as I do my own.'

'Still,' Harland pointed out, 'it would hardly help Carey to point that out to the police, would it?'

'Of course it would—it—' Her eyes widened. 'Oh!'

'As pretty a motive for Carey as you'd want to find,' David nodded, 'if his wife is taking jewelry from someone else.'

'Except,' Beatrice reminded him, 'that Carey wasn't there. He was selling Mrs George on a new campaign. And that reminds me of a queer thing. It can't have anything to do with Tony's death but during the party I found Mrs George going frantically through the drawer of Tony's dressing table. She looked desperate. And you remember the way she hung on, forcing her way out on the terrace when that scene went on over Tony and Miles? She was hanging around, trying to talk to Tony. And yet she was a new client. She'd never met Tony before. I know it doesn't make much sense,' she added lamely. 'It's just an unexplained thing.'

'Mrs George?' David asked. 'The smart-looking woman with the artificial smile? Who is she, anyhow?'

'Hazel George. She has a school of charm.'

David snapped his fingers. 'Got it! I knew she looked familiar. I've seen her around. She keeps house with Senator Packard.'

'Impossible,' Beatrice protested. 'The man must be seventy.'

'He has young ideas. Never could print it though,' David added regretfully. 'He was my paper's candidate and we looked after our own.'

Harland's eyes were shining. 'You are going to be the soundest investment of my life.'

'You ain't seen nothin' yet,' David promised him.

'Anyhow,' Beatrice said, 'Mrs George is out. Carey was with her at the time Tony was killed.'

'Any other candidates?'

'Miles Aldrich,' David said stubbornly.

'All right,' Harland said. 'You can start with Miles now. And while you're about it, look up the story of his brother's accident.'

A smile of satisfaction lighted David's face. 'This,' he declared, 'is going to be a pleasure.'

'Keep in touch with me. Better give me a ring as soon as you get anything. Tomorrow we'll be business-like and go into the sordid details of salary and so forth.'

'Oh, that,' David said with superb indifference, and he took his departure.

'And now that the young firebrand has gone,' Harland said, 'let's talk about Jennie.'

102

'Jennie couldn't have done it!' Beatrice exclaimed. 'Just because you saw her angry last night—I've known her for years and never saw her even ruffled before. She is always good-natured; cheery and hearty—you know the type. One of those earnest girls who go all out for community singing and folk dancing and girl scouts. She—'

'Steady,' he said. 'Take it easy, Beatrice. You do protest too much. Where was she this morning? Why did it take her so long to get her mother's message? And don't think the police won't find out about Jennie's quarrel with Tony over Miles. Why, she couldn't even conceal her antagonism when they began to question her.'

'But no one will tell the police about that quarrel,' Beatrice insisted eagerly. 'There were no outsiders—except Mrs George,' she added faintly. 'I'd forgotten Mrs George.'

'She is your job,' Harland said. 'I don't need to warn you to be diplomatic. You were born that way. But you might see whether you can find out what Tony had that Mrs George wanted so badly.' He added, 'What made you so sure Jennie saw Tony this morning—after you knew it wasn't Freda who had come downstairs?'

'I never said that,' Beatrice said quickly.

'My dear,' Harland pointed out patiently, 'it has been said in a dozen ways. You said it when you were so anxious to tell Mattheson that

Jennie hadn't been inside the apartment since the cocktail party. Her mother said it when she tried to protect her. Miles said it when he attempted to intimidate Mattheson—and incidentally, the lieutenant doesn't intimidate worth a hang. David said it when he risked his job to get there. Why do you all think it was Jennie?'

Beatrice tried to look away from his eyes but they held her. Other people had had the same experience of being neatly pinned to the wall by Harland's eyes without being able to extricate themselves.

'Shall I tell you?' he asked at length when she remained stubbornly silent. 'It was because something—the rustle of a skirt, the tap of a heel, perhaps even some perfume, told you that it was a woman on the stairs.'

She looked at him miserably and then her face lighted with relief. 'But, John,' she cried, 'it was after that—after the person stumbled going back up the stairs, that I felt someone look at me.'

'And no one was there?'

'There was someone,' she whispered in horror. 'There was someone.'

CHAPTER NINE

David pushed aside the last of the clippings and got up. They had given him no new facts on the death of Graham Aldrich. They all covered the same ground: a story on page one about the finding of his body, an account of the freak accident which had enabled a man with a broken neck to go home under his own power; a mention of the fight in the night club, modified, in most cases, to a mere disturbance. Most of the space was taken up—depending on the newspaper—with a list of Graham's clubs, or his checkered career as a playboy, or his family's social and financial background. They did not, David decided, say anything at all.

He went into the city room, feeling awkward and self-conscious. By now everyone must know he had been fired for refusing an assignment.

'Hi, Mack.' He perched on the side of a desk, and the rewrite man pushed back his eyeshade and blinked at him.

'Hi, David! Too damned bad—'

David cut him off. 'I was going to quit anyhow,' he lied. 'I suppose the old man got wind of it and wanted the satisfaction of getting in his jab first.'

The rewrite man blinked disillusioned eyes. 'That sounds like him,' he agreed. 'I envy you, getting out of this racket.' He would have worked for a newspaper if he had had to print it himself. 'Say,' he added as an after thought, 'you must have been caught short. Need a twenty?'

'Thanks.' David brushed the offer aside. He still had three dollars and eighty-five cents in his pocket. 'Right now I'm well heeled. As a matter of fact, I had a job waiting for me. Stepped right into it.'

'Yeah?' Mack said skeptically.

'I'm working with John Harland.'

The rewrite man straightened up. 'How do you rate a break like that?'

'Where did you come across him?' David countered.

'Not,' the rewrite man pointed out, 'through the nimble work of you reporters. But I keep my ear to the ground. Harland has a way of getting mixed up in the damnedest things. What's he on to now?'

'He's working on Tony Walker's murder.'

The rewrite man pulled a pad of paper toward him. 'Mrs Carey Walker? So it was murder.'

'Ask the cops.'

'You wouldn't hold out on your friends, would you?' Mack was righteously shocked.

David made a vulgar sound. 'Can you see me bringing in a nice juicy story for—' and he described the city editor graphically and in considerable detail.

'It might get your job back.'

'I have a job,' David said impatiently. 'I just dropped in to see you.'

'Missed us, I suppose. How long ago were you fired—four hours?'

'Well, as a matter of fact,' David admitted, 'I came in to look up some clippings. I see Tim Oleson covered the death of Graham Aldrich last year. How come the nightclub man covers a news story?'

'He was there when it happened. Fell right into his lap.'

'Where can I find him now?'

'At three in the afternoon? God knows. Probably at his apartment. He's a night-blooming plant.'

'Do you know where he lives?'

'I could find out.'

'Do that, will you, Mack?'

The rewrite man looked at him curiously and then lifted his phone. When he put it down he scrawled an address and handed it to David. 'Here it is, Sixty-seventh Street between Fifth and Madison. We seem to be doing all right by Oleson. I wonder how he rates that kind of money?'

Oleson lived on the second floor of a remodeled town house. David pressed the button and waited. Then he put his thumb on the bell and kept it there until the inner door clicked open.

The stairway was wide, with a curving white

railing; the hall gracious and furnished with fine old pieces. At the top of the stairs an irate man in gaudy pajamas stood in the open door and told him what he thought of him.

'I work nights,' he howled. 'I sleep days. Why can't I get that into anyone's head?'

Tim Oleson was short and chubby, with thinning blond hair and dark pouches under his eyes.

David grinned at him. 'Sorry, Oleson. They told me you'd be sore but I had to do it.'

'What do you want?'

'You were at the Club Royale the night Graham Aldrich was hurt, weren't you?'

'Oh.' The drowsiness vanished from Oleson's small, reddish eyes. 'And who the hell are you?'

'My name is Morehouse and we work for the same sheet,' David said breezily, and pushed his way past the man who blocked the doorway.

'Oh,' Oleson said again, and he added acidly, 'Can't I urge you to come in?'

'Well, so long as I am in.' David looked around. He whistled. 'They don't keep me in this style.'

'Possibly they are waiting until you acquire some manners.'

The apartment consisted of one huge room, with a miniature kitchenette and bath. Spectacular drapes covered the whole front wall, drawn to shut off the view of the street.

On one side there was a fireplace of colored marble, with a Chinese screen in front of it and gleaming fire tools in a polished metal container. Several deep couches, so low one had to lie on them; soft, low chairs, a radio phonograph with a television screen, a portable bar, were scattered around the big room, which still seemed almost empty. Against a wall there was an unmade couch bed.

The room was permeated with an odor David could not at first identify. At length he recognized it as a blend of paint, varnish and incense. The whole place, from the gleaming woodwork to the polished fire tongs, reeked of newness.

Oleson ran a fat hand over his uncombed hair. 'As long as the old man sent you, I'll give you ten minutes. I'll be with you,' and he went out.

David sprawled on one of the low couches. From the kitchenette came sounds indicating that Oleson was making some coffee; then the shower was turned on. David took a thick, initialed cigarette from a japanned box and lighted it from a strip of matches which also bore Oleson's initials. By the time he had crushed out his third cigarette Oleson returned, wearing a heavily brocaded satin dressing gown and looking refreshed and alert. He set down the tray, lowered himself cautiously onto a low divan, and poured some coffee. There was only one cup. Oleson was not a man to dispense hospitality to impecunious reporters.

The coffee splashed over the cup into the saucer and Oleson clucked in annoyance. He had pudgy hands, the nails too well kept, and at the moment his fingers had a slight tremor.

'So what the hell do you want?' he asked.

'I want to know what happened at the Club Royale the night Graham Aldrich got hurt.'

'Wait until I get some coffee inside me and I'll be more useful,' Oleson said.

'No hurry.'

Oleson took him at his word. He finished the cup of black coffee, poured another, and reached for one of the thick Egyptian cigarettes. Half lying on the deep divan, he thrust a couple of pillows under his head. The divan, the pose, the dressing gown, the incense, struck David as a setting for a bad play.

'Why come to me about Graham's death?'

'You covered the story.'

'Hell, I was there. What do you expect a news man to do? If you read the printed accounts, you know all I do about it.'

'Then you don't think there was anything queer about the way the guy died?'

'Queer?' Oleson yawned, a wide, convincing, contagious yawn, but the small eyes were bright and intent. 'Sure it was queer. The guy breaks his neck and never knows it and goes home before he collapses.'

'I suppose,' David suggested, 'there was no

question that his neck was broken at the club and not after he got home?'

Oleson yawned again. 'Oh, there was a question, all right. But it was just an accident. The doctors said it had happened before, a man with a broken neck living for some hours without knowing what had happened to him.'

David waited and Oleson went on. 'This is the way it happened. The Club Royale had a new dance team I was to cover that night and they gave me a ringside table. Graham Aldrich came in and he was high, noisy and troublesome. Spoiling for a fight. If he hadn't been an Aldrich they would have thrown him out, but he always more than paid for the trouble he caused. For a wonder, he was alone, and he began to make a nuisance of himself with a girl who was at the next table. Naturally, the girl's escort got sore and told him to cut it out. Aldrich threw something—a bottle, I think. Anyhow, his aim wasn't too good and he hit another character and there was a free for all. The other fellow knocked him down.'

As David looked at him expectantly, Oleson added, 'That's all I saw myself. The rest came out at the inquest. The manager had Graham picked up, put in a cab, and sent home. The cab driver helped him up to his door. He thought Graham was tight.'

David thought about it. 'Actually, then,' he said, 'there is no real evidence that the fight in the club was the one that broke Graham's neck. Or is there?'

'I've been answering all the questions,' Oleson pointed out. 'How about you answering some?'

'Fair enough—if I know the answers.'

'Why are you smelling around Graham Aldrich ten months after his death?'

'I'm working on the Tony Walker murder.'

'On the what? Jesus!' Oleson's coffee splashed onto his pajama legs. He leaped to his feet. 'The stuff's boiling!' He mopped up the coffee and sat down again. Considering his build and the low structure of the divan, this was a complicated operation. 'Sorry. I'm not at my best when I'm waked out of a sound sleep. What did you say happened to her?'

'Murdered this morning. Electrocuted.'

Oleson gave a horrified exclamation.

'Her husband is a public relations man, Walker-Comstock outfit. Do you know them?'

'I know the Walkers by sight,' Oleson said vaguely. 'Seen them around at theaters and night spots.' He got up again. 'Coffee all over that damn couch,' he said and moved to a chair. 'What has Tony Walker to do with Graham Aldrich?' he asked as he subsided into the chair with a grunt.

'I don't know,' David admitted.

'Another bright idea of the old man's, I suppose,' Oleson said tolerantly.

There was one thing sure, David thought. If he had not already lost his job, he'd have been

112

blown through the window after Oleson and the city editor compared notes.

'What are you trying to prove?' Oleson asked abruptly. 'That Graham Aldrich was all right when he left the club and that he had his neck broken later?'

'Could it have happened that way?'

Oleson took his time answering the question, pondering. 'No,' he decided at length, 'it couldn't. The police considered that angle, Aldrich influence or no Aldrich influence. And there were plenty of witnesses to the fight at the club. The doctors agreed his neck was broken there. And no evidence appeared that anyone got into the house after he reached home. Do you know that old mausoleum on Fifth? It would be as easy to break and enter as it would be to get into Tiffany's undetected.' He pressed out his cigarette on a jade ashtray. 'Are you after Miles Aldrich?'

'I'm after facts,' David said. 'You should know the old man well enough for that. But, after all, Miles profited by his brother's death.'

'Where do you get that?' Oleson protested. 'Their father left the bulk of the estate and its control to Miles, with a trust fund for Graham. The kid was a heel from way back and his father knew better than to allow him too much money. Graham's death didn't make Miles any richer.' Oleson yawned. 'What's supposed to be the connection between Graham's death and the murder of Mrs Walker?'

'Well,' David said in what he hoped was a cryptic tone, 'we have to look at all the angles.'

When it became apparent that David had nothing more to say, Oleson struggled out of his chair. 'Sorry I can't be of any more help. And now, if you'll get the hell out, I'm going back to bed.'

'Oh, one thing more. Who was the guy who tangled with Graham at the club?'

'I have no idea. Remember, no one suspected that night the guy had been hurt seriously. So far as I know, the other character never came forward. Can't say I blame him.' Oleson flapped his hand in languid farewell and trundled toward his bed. 'By the way, how was Mrs Walker electrocuted?'

'Radio dropped in her bathtub.'

'My, my, what will they think of next?' Oleson sank down on the side of the couch and untied the cord of his dressing gown. 'Well, you can take my word for it, that let's Miles out. That guy never saw an undressed woman in his life. And where in hell was her husband?'

'Out with a client. Airtight alibi.'

Oleson nodded and stretched out on the bed. 'Beastly things, radios. Close the door behind you, stinker.'

David let himself out and pulled the door toward him. There was a sound inside the room and he held the door open a crack. Oleson was at the telephone, dialing a number.

In a moment he said in a low, urgent tone, 'Mr Aldrich, please. Tell him that it is important.'

CHAPTER TEN

Beatrice pushed open the violet door and walked into a small reception room done in black and white squares, its walls mirrored. At first, there seemed to be half a dozen slim, haggard, smartly dressed women and half a dozen receptionists. Then the flesh and blood receptionist looked up with a bright smile and caroled, 'How may I serve madam?'

'I'd like to see Mrs George.'

The receptionist was unhappy. 'Mrs George,' she mourned, 'sees people only by appointment.' Her eyes brightened. All was not lost. 'But our analysts can advise madam in regard to her needs. I can see at a glance it isn't reducing. Not with madam's figure. Our hair stylist? Our make-up consultant?'

Beatrice glanced uneasily in the mirror. What, she wondered, was wrong with her make-up? 'I must see Mrs George,' she said. 'Tell her it is Miss Comstock and very important.' As the receptionist hesitated, Beatrice added with assurance, 'She'll see me.'

The receptionist pushed open a padded-satin door and went out with an undulating movement of her hips. On impulse, Beatrice followed, forestalled her as she was about to tap on a door painted silver, brushed past her and went in. With a helpless shrug of her shoulders the girl went back to her desk.

The silver door swung noiselessly onto a deep-carpeted room whose predominating color was a soft peach that was kind to aging faces. Mrs George sat at a kidney shaped desk, her back to the door, talking over the telephone. Her voice was loud, angry.

'Do you think it's doing me any good? Ruin the business, that's all...' Her voice became placating. 'I know, Sweetie pie. I'll think of something. You leave it to Hazel. You know who loves you, don't you, Honey? You just leave it to Hazel ... Bye now.'

She put down the telephone and Beatrice reached back to close the door behind her. Mrs George swung around in her chair. For a moment the two women measured one another in silence and then Beatrice smiled and came forward with her hand outstretched.

'Good afternoon, Mrs George,' she said with the big smile that gave her face so much warmth. 'I hoped you wouldn't mind my dropping in like this. I came—' she paused for a moment and then added with directness—'I came because we are two women who have been hurt by the same person. I couldn't help myself but perhaps I can help you.'

'I don't know,' Mrs George said, 'what you are talking about.'

'I think you do,' Beatrice told her. 'I am talking about Tony Walker. As you must have learned from that telephone call, she died this morning.'

The Streamlined Job was falling apart before her eyes. Under the careful make-up, Hazel George's skin was livid. Her stately carriage sagged. But the stuff she was made of was hard. She was a fighter.

'Just what are you trying to do, Miss Comstock? If you think you can blackmail me—'

'Blackmail!' Beatrice sank down facing Mrs George. 'So that's it! The little fiend. The unspeakable little fiend. Look here, Mrs George. We might as well be honest with each other. I've always known Tony was no good. Maybe I shouldn't speak ill of the dead but she has left trouble behind her—plenty of it. She hurt too many people. You don't need to tell me what she did to you if you don't want to.'

'But my dear Miss Comstock!' The careful articulation, the cultivated accent had been restored. 'I don't understand.'

'No, I don't think you do. Tony was murdered. That's an ugly thing and the police are digging for motive. And motive,' she quoted Harland, 'is the only thing that can never be concealed. If you'll trust me, I think I can help you. After all, my office is in the penthouse. If she took something of yours, perhaps I can find it for you.'

'For me?' Mrs George suggested, 'or for the police?'

'For you. No matter how strong your motive for disliking Tony, Mrs George, we both know—we could prove—that you had nothing to do with her death. You are safe enough. No, I just wanted to spare you any unfortunate publicity if I can.'

'Why should there be any publicity?'

'Because it is murder,' Beatrice said patiently.

'Why don't they pick up the sister-in-law with the wrong clothes? I'm no fool, Miss Comstock. I know why you're here. Motive? Jennie Walker had it, all right, with Mrs Walker taking her boy friend and the Aldrich money too. She was killing mad, all right, and she didn't care who knew about it.'

'And yet, if that story comes out,' Beatrice said hesitantly, almost regretfully, 'I would have to point out that Tony had injured other people. If I were to find what you were looking for yesterday, I'd have to turn it over to the police. You can see that, can't you?'

Mrs George saw it. 'All right,' she said, 'you win. As the saying goes, we women have to stick together. It's like this. My boy friend is Senator Packard, and he's the openhanded kind, a heart as big as all outdoors. And as he says, the best is none too good for me. So he set me up here and now and then he wants me to have a little present. Like he says, he won't be

118

here always and I've got to think of the future.'

'Tony didn't steal an emerald necklace from you, did she?' Beatrice asked in excitement.

'Lord, no! Packy isn't made of money. Oh, I get it. She took things from other people too.'

'She took things from other people,' Beatrice said grimly.

'No,' Mrs George said, 'it wasn't jewelry. It was just a sheet of paper. Packy wrote a list of my investments so I'd have the stuff straight on my tax report. Only he'd done it on his letterhead. He's usually careful, poor old Sugar!'

'But why should Tony have come here in the first place?'

'Professional visit. Her face was a mess. Looks to me like someone beat the bejesus out of her—more power to whoever it was. She wanted to know if I could cover up the marks on her face with make-up for the party, but that stuff is out of my line. There were a couple of specialists for it. I don't have the equipment. So she thought it over and laughed and said, all right, she'd just stay as she was. It seemed to tickle her for some reason.'

The receptionist tapped at the door and crossed to the desk with the gliding step of a model.

'Lieutenant Mattheson of the Homicide department,' she murmured, and then added in her natural Brooklynese, 'But if you ask me, he's just a policeman in disguise.'

'Send him in when I ring,' Mrs George said. 'It will be just a couple of minutes.' When the girl had gone out, she asked Beatrice, 'Do you think you can find that paper before the police do?'

'I'll find it if I have to take the whole duplex to pieces.'

Mrs George placed the palms of her broad hands flat on the table and leaned forward, her eyes raking Beatrice's face. 'You wouldn't double cross me, would you?'

'Good heavens, no!'

'It wouldn't be smart to try it.' Mrs George's voice was flat and ugly.

What am I doing here, talking to a woman of this kind, Beatrice thought with distaste, but she spoke civilly enough. 'I'll keep my side of the bargain. What about Jennie Walker?'

'Jennie?' Mrs George said dryly. 'Oh, sure.' She laughed. 'Don't give it a moment's thought.'

Beatrice met the knowing eyes and forced herself to hold out her hand to seal the bargain.

'You're a good egg,' Mrs George said. 'A real sport. And just to show my appreciation I'll have Pierre—he's my best operator—give you the works. It'll take quite a while and the lieutenant—' she snorted—'"a policeman in disguise." My God, is that girl dumb!—he'll be gone by then. No use letting him get nosy about why you are here.'

120

*   *   *

For several hours Harland had tried to concentrate on the book he was reading, but something nagged at him, something he could not quite get hold of, and he gave up. David had telephoned once to say that he was on the track of Graham Aldrich but he had to see a man and he'd be calling later.

Harland put down his book and rested his head against the red-leather chair, his narrow head, long nose and brilliant eyes making him resemble an intelligent greyhound. His restless mind tried to track down the thought, the memory, whatever it was that eluded him.

At length he gave it up. Memory was a jade; escaping so long as you pursue her; coming of her own accord if you neglect her.

He put on his hat and left the house, walking aimlessly toward Sixth Avenue. He bought the evening papers and strolled back to Fifth Avenue, brooding. One of the few remaining two-decker buses lumbered past. People were already having cocktails at the sidewalk cafés. Harland watched them for a few moments and then sauntered back to his house. Under a tree in his garden there was a little shade and he settled down with the newspapers.

You don't know what people think until you know what they read, the kind of nourishment they feed their brains, Harland had often declared, so he read everything from the *Sun* to

121

the tabloids. The experience was a salutary one and humbling to the spirit. He laid the papers in a neat pile on the seat beside him and picked up the top one.

BRIDE ELECTROCUTED IN PENTHOUSE

screamed the headlines, and below there was a picture of Tony with her triangular face, strange eyes, and voluptuous body, generously revealed in a scanty bathing suit.

Page three contained a picture of the living-room of the penthouse with a glimpse of the bar and a shot of the bathroom where Tony had been found. For a long time Harland studied that picture. It showed the ledge where the radio had stood, with arrows pointing to the grooves into which the radio had fitted. It showed racks of monogrammed bathtowels, and other towels strewn over the floor, one of them lying in a pool of water. It showed glass shelves cluttered with bottles and jars and atomizers. In a small oval inset there was a cabinet portrait of Carey, looking handsome and sincere.

The reporters had played up the penthouse, the fact that Tony had been married only a few months, the electrocution. These were all sure-fire tabloid items. Lieutenant Mattheson was playing them close to his chest. There was no direct statement that the death was murder, though the implications were clear enough.

122

The heart-broken husband was in a state of collapse. The tragedy had been discovered by a friend of the family. Mattheson, Harland decided, was a model of discretion.

Then his heavy eyebrows shot up. Present at the time the police arrived was John Harland, author of *Man's Worst Enemy*, a man of mystery whose spectacular life was in surprising contrast to the scholarly understatement of his books. The distinguished psychologist was a friend of the family.

Harland put down the tabloid and looked blankly at the slanting shadows across the garden. There was, he decided, considerably more to Lieutenant Mattheson than met the eye.

As he reached for the next paper he became conscious that his housekeeper was hovering near him.

'Yes, Mrs Larsen.'

'It's the telephone. The lady won't give her name but she says it's important.'

Harland glanced down at the newspaper and sighed. It was beginning. The infrequent appearances of his name in connection with some story had always brought a deluge of telephone calls.

The woman at the other end of the line was breathless with excitement. From the incoherent jumble of words that she poured out, Harland gathered that: (1) she had seen his name in the paper; (2) she knew it because his book was on the best-seller shelf of her lending library though personally she preferred a good romance; (3) she had seen the girl who died; (4) she didn't like to get mixed up with the police because you never know; (5) unless she imparted her information without delay she would fall victim to self-induced spontaneous combustion.

Harland sorted it all out and then suggested that he call upon the lady. Every sensational crime had its sequel of crank letters and telephone calls and sometimes one of them paid off. There was an awkward pause and then she asked, in some embarrassment, whether she could come to him instead. 'It's my daughter-in-law,' she explained. 'She thinks I'm an old busybody and anyhow she doesn't want to get messed up in a police case.'

Harland was waiting at the curb when the taxi drew up and a stout, cheerful looking elderly woman got out. It seemed to Harland at times that every elderly woman in New York was starved for someone to talk to and all of them, by some sixth sense, recognized him as a natural victim. He might struggle but he never escaped. Sooner or later, they managed to unload their whole family history on him. The alarming thing was that invariably he began to be interested. He had become involved in the damnedest things because he listened to the gossip of old women, and then got to wondering.

This woman was in her middle sixties, heavy, with a surprisingly unlined face for her age. Her hair was iron gray, pulled back into an uncompromising knot on the back of her head. She looked Harland over candidly and then nodded approval.

'So you're Mr Harland,' she said. 'I wish my daughter-in-law could get a look at you, after the things she said. A real distinguished looking gentleman.' A comment that for once in his life found Harland at a loss. 'I'm Mrs Jacobs.'

She exclaimed as he led her through the garden and into the big living-room where Mrs Larsen had prepared a pitcher of iced tea with mint floating on it.

'Well,' Mrs Jacobs declared, 'this is real nice. But all those books. What would a person do with them? And such a job to dust!' She sipped her tea, nodded her head, and began, 'You could have knocked me over when I saw the picture in the paper of that poor girl!'

'A sad thing.' Harland shook his head. 'Did you know her?'

'No,' Mrs Jacobs said, 'but I saw her just the other night. It's the same girl, all right. There can't be two with those three-cornered eyes. And she was sitting at the next table, as close as I am to you.'

'Really!' Harland was giving her his full attention now, something no man had done in twenty years. 'When was that?'

'Tuesday,' she said, and Harland's interest was intensified. Tuesday had been the night of the burglary.

'Sure of the day?' he asked her.

'I should say.' The woman's false teeth did not quite fit and she had some difficulty with her sibilants. 'It was my birthday and my son and his wife took me out to dinner to celebrate. In my time, we had birthday celebrations at home but my son's wife doesn't like to cook. So we went to this restaurant and not a thing on the menu under three dollars. I give you my word. Spending my son's money like water. Of course, he is doing well, but easy come, easy go. Put a little aside for your old age, I tell her. Where would I be now if I'd gone around spending three dollars for dinner? But it goes in one ear and out the other with Lida.' She took a deep breath. 'So there was this girl at the very next table.'

'Alone?'

'No. There was a man with her. Older than she was and run to seed. Unhealthy looking and half starved, as though she'd picked him off a breadline.'

'Could you describe him?'

'Thin, dark, a nervous tic to his eyelids, under thirty, but he'd lived enough for sixty.' She thought for a moment, eyes half closed, and added that the man was approximately five feet eight, narrow shoulders, and weighed about a hundred and twenty-eight pounds. 'Skinny build like you, only not so much so, if you know what I mean. He wore a blue suit, shiny and unpressed, and a blue and white striped necktie.'

Harland smiled. 'What a witness you would make! It's rare to see a person who really uses his eyes. I've always contended that people don't observe what they look at.'

'No more they do. It comes of not paying proper attention,' the woman agreed with him. 'Now if there's one thing more than another I pride myself on, it's that I notice things. But then I'm interested.' Her voice subsided to a grumble. 'Those who aren't interested in more'n themselves don't see beyond their noses.' The grumble was a matter of principle rather than conviction. She had too good a digestion to be genuinely ill tempered.

Harland firmly pulled her back to the subject at hand. 'So even at your own birthday party you took an interest in strangers.'

'Well, it was really Lida called my attention. She got mad because my son kept staring at this girl. So we all noticed her. She was wearing a white evening dress and that started another squabble between Lida and Paul. He said it was simple, and Lida said wasn't that just like a man; always taken in. She'd seen a dress just like it priced at a hundred and eighty-five dollars; though what she thought she was doing, looking at that type dress, I'm sure I

127

don't know, when before she married Paul she was glad to pick her clothes off the racks on Fourteenth Street. And then she said anyhow there was nothing simple about a girl who wore emeralds.'

'So there were emeralds,' Harland said softly.

'I'm telling you.' The old lady wagged her head. 'Simply gorgeous.'

'Could you hear anything they said?'

'Part of the time they were arguing, but he was crazy mad about her.' She nodded her head. 'Crazy mad,' she repeated, as though she could not improve on her own phrase. 'Just sick when he found out she was married. And then it was, "Oh, Alvin darling," and all that.'

'She called him Alvin?'

The woman nodded. 'But she'd jilted him. You could see that, all right. Not that I blame her. Not good enough, he wasn't. And it kind of tickled Lida to see the girl pay for the dinner. "At least," she says to Paul afterwards, "I may not wear a hundred and eighty-five dollar dress," she says, "but I don't have to pay the dinner check either," she says.'

'So Mrs Walker paid for the dinner, did she?'

'Oh, she could afford it all right. She pulled out a big wad of bills. I remember thinking with that type man she was taking a risk to show she had so much cash on her, I mean, you never know what people will do, if you know what I mean.'

'You make it so clear,' Harland assured her.

Mrs Jacobs settled herself more comfortably. It was real nice to have a good talk like this, and about an electrocution too. An electrocution, you might say, that had almost grazed you, having sat right next to the corpse only a couple of days before the Deed was Done.

Mrs Jacobs sipped her tea, grateful for the cool sound of ice against the silver goblet, grateful for the sound of traffic coming muted through the garden and the noise of children screaming as they played. As she grew older she needed the reassurance of life moving about her, the comforting awareness of her own quick body, particularly when she spoke of the dead.

'It makes you think, doesn't it?' she sighed. 'I mean, it all goes to show that you never can tell.'

'I wonder if you know,' Harland said, 'how valuable this information of yours would be to the police. Would you be willing to repeat your story to them in the interests of justice?'

'Well, now,' she considered. 'And I didn't get my hair set this week.' She eyed him shrewdly. 'Someone killed her and you think that little rat did it.'

'We mustn't jump to conclusions,' Harland warned her. 'That's a terrible charge when you think things through to the end.'

She thought them through to the end and

nodded soberly. 'I'll go right now if you want me to.'

'You are very kind.'

'Well, I don't know. Like you say, it's only my duty. And anyhow,' she added, 'the girl was young and lovely and she's dead.'

And that, Harland thought, was the kindest epitaph Tony Walker was likely to have.

CHAPTER ELEVEN

When the old lady had repeated her story to Mattheson and taken her departure, the lieutenant came back to his desk and made some telephone calls. Then he pulled out a battered pack of cigarettes, offered one to Harland and helped himself. He met Harland's quizzical eyes and grinned.

'I figured we'd get some information as soon as we had the girl's picture plastered all over the papers,' he said. 'Someone was bound to have known or seen her somewhere.'

'You also figured,' Harland murmured, 'that plastering my name all over the papers would bring information which people wouldn't take to the police.'

'Naturally,' Mattheson said blandly. 'I use what I've got and as long as you're in the picture somewhere—just what is your interest in this case, Mr Harland?'

Harland spread his bony hands in a vague gesture but his eyes were alert and his nervous energy made him seem as live as a time fuse.

'I'm interested in people. My field is humanics. In a way, it's a new field, because it means the study of the whole man, his biology, his chemistry, his psychology. If we could ever learn why men behave as they do, we'd have a fighting chance to make this a good world to live in. In a way, crime is a most effective revelation of character because there is something tangible to work with—a strong play of cause and effect. But I am not,' Harland added with a hint of self-mockery, 'an amateur detective. I don't get in the way of the police. All I am after is to try to find out why people resort to crime.'

'You got in on this one without wasting any time,' Mattheson commented.

'Miss Comstock telephoned me.' Briefly, Harland described knowing her as a child and her asking him to the cocktail party with the idea that he might become a client of Walker-Comstock.

Mattheson cocked an eyebrow. 'I've always been under the impression that you didn't court publicity. That Jean Clark disappearance, for instance, never got into the papers.' He studied the tip of his cigarette. 'And what do you make of Mrs Jacobs' story?'

Harland shrugged. 'There doesn't seem to be any reason to believe she was lying.'

'No,' Mattheson drawled, 'and yet it's odd, you know. We start with the idea that Mrs Walker knows no one in New York. Then sister Jennie gets involved and suddenly there's an unidentified stranger acting suspicious.'

'Am I to understand,' Harland asked in surprise, 'that you aren't going to make a search for this man Alvin?'

Mattheson slid back on his spine and pulled at his lip. 'Oh, we'll look for him. He seems to have been the burglar who beat up Mrs Walker.' He glanced at Harland. 'Don't misunderstand me. I'm not trying to do this the hard way. Nine times out of ten it is the obvious person who is guilty and everything points to Mrs Walker's ex-boy friend. But I can't ignore other possibilities.'

'For instance?'

'For instance, an emerald necklace Mrs Walker's family apparently did not know about. An ex-wife who happened to find the body. A sister-in-law who hated her like hell. A husband who isn't telling all he knows. Not by a long shot. But we'll haul in our elusive friend Alvin and maybe we'll learn more about Antonia Smith, Chicago, than we've found out so far. Though we've already got one nice item. It appears from the autopsy that Mrs Walker took dope. Makes it interesting, doesn't it?'

'Unexpected,' Harland admitted.

Mattheson meditated for a moment, pushing out his rubbery lip. 'A funny set-up,' he said as though to himself. 'First wife and second wife all palsy-walsy.'

Harland explained the partnership as convincingly as he could. 'And it was purely a business relationship. The fact that the duplex was also used as the Walker-Comstock office was simply a matter of convenience.'

Mattheson wasn't buying it. 'It just doesn't work out. Not two wives getting along. Never heard of a case.'

'This one did.'

'And one wife is dead.' Which gave Mattheson the last word.

Harland, however, was in no hurry to leave. 'As long as you've put my name in the papers as bait,' he remarked, 'you might let me string along on this.'

'Glad to,' Mattheson said promptly. 'You have a reputation for being able to pull the rabbit out of the hat.'

Harland smiled. 'No tricks.'

'So long,' Mattheson said, 'as it is the right rabbit.'

'And no favorites,' Harland promised.

'Suppose the rabbit looks like Miss Comstock or Jennie Walker?'

'For the moment,' Harland said, 'I'm not going to borrow trouble by supposing anything of the sort. Miss Comstock put the case against herself more strongly than the facts justify. Her interest centers in the business.'

'She is a clever lady,' Mattheson admitted. 'But she could be a liar. And if she is, nobody came down the stairs this morning, and that, my friend, leaves her holding the bag.'

'What's the next step?'

'There are plenty of lines to follow up. I've got a man checking the restaurant where Mrs Jacobs saw Tony Walker with the man Alvin. We're following up the emerald necklace. Got some men checking the jewelry shops. We're sending out a description of the missing boy friend, checking on the whole Walker outfit, and that house the Walkers live in. Someone may have seen whoever it was who came up there this morning. An automatic elevator and no doorman, so it's not likely. Still,' he added cheerfully, 'people usually are seen. And we're trying to get some information from Chicago about Antonia Smith. I'd like to know a lot more about her. What did you make of the girl?'

Harland considered the question. 'She filled my mind with ideas but I'm not sure what they are.' Then he decided that a police station was a poor place to quote Alice.

'She must have been a knockout when she was alive.'

'Of course,' Harland reminded him, 'I saw her only once, when her face was puffy and discolored from that beating. But I had a strong impression that she was more than attractive; she was genuinely alluring.' He

134

added slowly, 'And she was probably the kind who robbed blind beggars and stole candy from children. She had a talent for striking where the defenses were down.'

'You didn't like her,' Mattheson said.

'It would have given me infinite pleasure,' Harland admitted, 'to beat her within an inch of her life.'

'Someone else,' the lieutenant pointed out, 'had the same idea.'

The telephone rang and Mattheson scooped it up. He talked briefly and then grinned at Harland. 'That was the man who checked the restaurant where Mrs Jacobs saw Mrs Walker. The waiter remembered them both. He described the same man Mrs Jacobs did and he swears Mrs Walker was wearing an emerald necklace. Also he noticed that the boy friend had contracted pupils. He may have been in on the dope end of this business.'

The phone rang again and this time he talked longer. When he set down the telephone Harland knew that once more the lieutenant had been dealt an ace in the hole.

'We've run down the jeweler who sold the emerald necklace,' he said. 'And here's one that will surprise you. Know who bought it? Mrs Walker herself. The jeweler identified the picture from the newspaper. He sold the necklace on Monday.' The detective made some meaningless scrawls on a piece of paper and added slowly, 'Fifteen thousand dollars it

135

cost—she exaggerated a bit—but the funny part is that she paid cash.'

Harland's eyes glowed as though candles had been lighted behind them. 'It would be interesting to know where that money came from.'

Mattheson nodded. 'If there's big money around anywhere we'll get on the track of it. Bound to crop up somewhere. If Aldrich wasn't the kind he is, I'd say you wouldn't have to look farther for the money.' He reflected for a moment. 'Could be,' he added, 'that Aldrich is the reason his fiancée didn't like Mrs Walker much.' He caught Harland's expression and shook his head. 'No, you're wrong. I'm not going easy on Aldrich because of his influence. It's his reputation. Sir Galahad out of Carrie Nation. It just won't wash.'

A large policeman with a stony face came into the room. 'I'm Sheehan. You want me?'

'Yes. About your report on the robbery at the Walker penthouse.'

'That's what I figured after I saw the papers. Well, there's not much to add to the report. I was on the prowl car when the call came. Mrs Walker was alone in the apartment. She said this burglar had broken in, stole a necklace, and got out again. She didn't even get a look at him. That's *her* story. The whole set-up smelled.'

'How?'

'Well, her husband got there while I was

checking. I could see he didn't believe a word his wife said either. First place, no one could have broken in the way she said. The duplex was as close to being burglar-proof as it could be. Unless the burglar dropped by parachute onto the terrace, there were just two ways in, the front door and the service entrance that the servants use, both on the upper floor of the duplex. The key was in the lock and the chain in place at the service entrance. The front door had a special lock that hadn't been tampered with. There were only four keys and all accounted for.'

Sheehan looked up to see whether they were following him. 'Another thing, while Walker and I were checking the locks, this babe made like she was doing her face and scattered powder all over the top of the dressing table and then wiped it up. Because why? She was afraid of fingerprints. Then this necklace she said she lost. I saw Walker's face and I'll swear it was the first time he ever heard of it. He didn't know whether to laugh or cuss.'

Matheson nodded thoughtfully. 'We've traced her movements that evening. She dined in a restaurant with a character named Alvin and she was wearing the emeralds. It's not hard to figure the rest. He was hard up; she was flashing a lot of cash. Either the guy came home with her or followed later and she let him in. He stole the necklace and she wanted it back but was afraid to say she knew him.'

Sheehan nodded. 'That all fits with what I saw.'

'But why,' Harland asked, 'did the fellow beat her up? She couldn't have put up that hard a fight.'

'I wouldn't call that a beating,' Sheehan protested. 'She showed us the marks—and then some.' He whistled appreciatively. 'Nothing exclusive about that jane.' He became official again. 'There were only a couple of fingermarks where he grabbed her shoulder.'

'A couple of fingermarks!' Mattheson said. 'I got a good look at the body after they lifted her out of the tub. Her face was a mess, swollen and discolored. There were bruises on her body too. Doc says they were all made a couple of days ago.' He brought his fist down on the table. 'If this bird she called Alvin didn't beat her up, then who did?'

*　　　*　　　*

A description of the man known as Alvin was going out over the teletype. Radio cars were picking it up. Policemen were watching the stations, the airports, the water front. The narcotics squad were checking the known dope peddlers. Stool pigeons were being questioned. A gigantic net was spread across New York in the hope of catching one small fish.

With his eyes nearly shut, it seemed to Alvin

138

that the children's sailboats on the pond in Central Park were life-size. He could ride in one of them, drifting straight off across the pond, across the park, to open water where he was free. Where there was nothing to haunt him. A sailboat and a fresh breeze and a blue sky. And Tony laughing beside him. Tony's mouth melting under his. But Tony wouldn't be there.

And he couldn't go without Tony. There wasn't strength enough in a man to leave her. Or pride enough to keep him from crawling back, listening to her mocking insults, and knowing that this pain was nothing to her. That even if he could tell her about it she would neither understand nor care. And there was no escape from this hell of wanting, so long as Tony lived. How could he love a woman so much that it was torment and yet hate her at the same time?

Out of the corner of his eye Alvin saw the shadow. There was someone standing beside the bench. His heart lurched. Tony! But it couldn't be Tony. It would never be Tony. Never again. He looked up from under the brim of his hat. It was a policeman. He got up shakily and moved on. He seemed to have been moving on forever. Wherever he sat, sooner or later there was a policeman and he moved on. Otherwise they would lock him up. Vagrancy.

They would lock him up. Alvin shambled along the path muttering to himself and behind him he heard the laughter of the children who were watching him. He swung around savagely.

They saw his distorted face and took to their heels.

Alvin went on again. Locked you up, that was what happened. And there was no way of getting a shot. Then you began to shake. The way he was shaking now. He had to have it. He had to have it. He had to have it. Now. He couldn't wait any longer.

After a furtive look around, he sat down on another bench. On the seat beside him there was a screwed-up cigarette package. He picked it up with shaking fingers and smoothed it out. Sometimes people overlooked a cigarette when they threw the package away. He prodded inside with a finger. There was a cigarette, twisted, but still a whole cigarette. He lighted it and a wave of dizziness washed through his head. That was because he had not had a cigarette for days, because he had not eaten since—when had he eaten, anyhow?

For the twentieth time he went through his pockets. Soiled handkerchiefs, some loose tobacco, a torn stamp, a keyring whose keys unlocked no doors any more. There wasn't a penny. Not one he could drop in a slot for a piece of chocolate.

But there was the necklace. It lay across the palm of his grimy hand, dazzling in the sunlight. It meant food and cigarettes and coffee. It meant a drink and a bed and a shot. Oh, God, he had to have it! He had to have it!

'It won't do you any good,' Tony said sharply, and Alvin jumped, but there was no one in sight. Tony kept talking to him but she was never there. She'd never be there. Never. Never.

'Why don't you let me alone?' he yelled, and the pigeons, walking delicately along the path on rosy feet, took off with a rapid beating of wings.

The cigarette was so short that it burned his fingers, but he took one more long pull before he dropped it. At the first exit, he left the park and started east. On Third Avenue he turned north. His feet burned from the hot pavement. His head was reeling. There were flashes across his eyes. At length he saw the pawnshop sign.

For all his frantic impatience, he paused for a moment, looking through the mesh protecting the window at the objects other people had disposed of in their time of need: watches and rings and a variety of musical instruments, mantel clocks and vases and Spanish shawls.

A bell jangled as he pushed open the door and went in. The man behind the counter was in shirt sleeves, a pair of glasses pushed up on his forehead. He studied Alvin's face but made no comment. He waited.

Alvin laid the gleaming necklace on the counter. 'How much?' he asked.

The pawnbroker shot a sharp glance at Alvin, adjusted a light and put a jeweler's glass in his eye, inspecting the necklace.

'How much would you expect?' he asked mildly, and Alvin relaxed.

'Five hundred dollars,' he said.

Was that too much to ask? Was it too little? How could you be expected to know what to ask? The pawnbroker did not reveal anything.

'Just a moment,' he said, and he went behind a curtain at the back of the shop.

As easy as that, Alvin thought. As easy as that. I could have asked for more. Maybe a lot more. Five hundred dollars. He had never had that much money at one time. It made him feel free. With five hundred dollars he could go anywhere, do anything. First, he would get something to eat and a drink and cigarettes. Then he would find a druggist and get a shot. How had he happened to lose the address of the doctor who would fix him up? When he had had the shot he would get his suit pressed and maybe buy a new shirt. He'd get a suitcase so he could rent a decent room. Then—*what was taking so long?* Why didn't the fellow come back?

Alvin heard the telephone click softly back on its cradle, snatched up the necklace and raced for the door. It jangled as he opened it and he felt that the ringing of the bell could be heard all over Third Avenue. An elevated train rattled by, covering the sound, and Alvin dashed up the stairs to the elevated platform. He found himself pushing against the turnstile. Then he remembered that he had no money.

Standing behind a signboard, he peered over the railing, down onto the street. He saw the pawnbroker come out and look up and down the sidewalk, saw the arrival of a radio car. He couldn't get away on the train and he did not dare go down the stairs to the street.

Another train rumbled in and the passengers got out. A sharp-voiced woman with a baby in one arm and a bundle in the other, two small children clinging to her skirts, edged her way off the train.

'Now you stay close to me,' she said shrilly. 'Come back here, Harry. Wait for Sally.'

Alvin took off his hat. 'I'll take the baby down for you,' he offered, 'so you can look after the others. What a lovely family.'

'Well, that's awfully kind.' She handed him the baby and the bundle, took the two children and they went down the stairs.

From the landing halfway down Alvin could see the radio car and the pawnbroker still standing in his doorway. It was like walking deliberately into the waiting arms of the law.

'Are you going far?' he asked in desperation as they reached the foot of the stairs and the mother reached for her baby.

'Just half a block, thank goodness.'

'Let me take the baby.'

'Well, I'm sure I don't know what to say.'

She trotted at his side, jerking the two older children along, keeping up a constant flood of conversation. 'Don't lag so, Sally. Mama's got to get home. Yes, I know it's a police car, Harry.' She smiled shyly at Alvin. 'I declare my arms are tired from carrying that baby. He's gained another three pounds. They sure grow fast. Harry, I tell you I don't know what the police car's waiting for. No, don't go bothering the cops. You come along with mama.'

The pawnshop was only a few yards away. 'Harry,' Alvin said, 'you heard what your mother told you.'

They walked past the pawnshop where the manager stood in the open door talking to a policeman. Alvin held the baby high against his shoulder so his face could not be seen. Neither man glanced at them as they were washed past on a wave of the mother's chatter.

'I'm sure I don't know how to thank you,' she said at her doorway.

'P-p-pleasure,' Alvin said, his teeth chattering, touched his hat, and took the first turning toward Second Avenue, his heart pounding. For all the heat, his body was clammy with a cold sweat.

'It won't do you any good,' Tony screamed at him and he snarled, 'Shut up, can't you? Shut up!'

A woman hurrying along the street looked at him and then veered toward the curb. Alvin did not see her. He saw nothing but a girl with a

144

triangular face. 'Go away,' he muttered. 'Go away and let me alone.'

The drugstore on Second Avenue was dingy and, except for a boy having a coke at the fountain, there were no customers. Alvin found the proprietor standing in front of a revolving fan that gave a wheeze and a nervous jerk each time it turned.

'What can I do for you?' the druggist asked.

Alvin told him in a whisper.

'Where's your prescription?'

He shook his head.

'Sorry,' the druggist said.

'Please,' Alvin said desperately, 'I've got to have it.'

'I can't help you. I'm not going to get into trouble with the law.'

'Look!' Alvin held out the necklace. 'Give me what I need. I got to have it. I can't wait. You can keep the necklace. See, I'm giving it to you.'

'What is this?' the druggist said in a loud voice. 'What do you think I am? I've got a good mind—'

Alvin did not hear the rest. He was out in the street again, the necklace dangling from his fingers. He shoved it into his pocket. The druggist would report him. He'd have to hurry. God, he said to himself. God. God. Oh, please. Oh, please.

CHAPTER TWELVE

Beatrice put her key in the lock and opened the door as quietly as she could. She stood listening. There were no voices from the kitchen. At four in the afternoon the servants should be in their own quarters. It would be another half hour before Mrs Harris came up to start her preparations for dinner.

On tiptoe, Beatrice crossed the foyer and opened the door to the living-room. It was empty. There was no one on the terrace. The police had gone. Back in the foyer again she listened at the top of the stairs. There was no sound of movement down below and yet some instinct made her stoop over and slip off her shoes. Holding them in one hand she went down noiselessly, the marble stairs cool beneath her stockinged feet.

The reception room and office were empty. Again she stopped to listen but there was no sound. She went swiftly down the hall, past the closed door of Carey's room to Tony's. For a moment her hand tightened on the knob and then she turned it and went in.

Obviously, the police had finished with the room. The bed had been made; the clothes, carelessly strewn over the floor, had been picked up; the dressing table was in order. Through the open door of the bathroom,

146

Beatrice saw that it too had been set to rights. The water had been mopped up, the used towels were gone. So was the radio.

For a moment she looked around her, remembering. She began to shake and she forced herself into some kind of control. There was no horror, none at all. No hint that a girl had died here only a few hours before. I never realized, she thought, that the dead leave so little trace. She's just—gone.

Get on with it, she told herself. Her eyes traveled around the bathroom. There was no place where anything could have been hidden. She went back into the bedroom and sat down at the dressing table. Without touching anything. She simply looked around, thinking about Tony. If Mrs George was right, Tony had been a blackmailer. And a thief. Somewhere she had hidden the paper on which the indiscreet Senator Packard had listed Mrs George's investments. A single sheet of paper would not be difficult to hide. But perhaps there were other things. If Tony had stolen the paper it was because she was an opportunist, grasping at whatever came her way.

All the time, Beatrice thought, I knew there was something wrong, horribly, fundamentally wrong. Because Tony was the kind of girl you'd expect to talk about herself and she never did. It didn't fit—unless she had something to conceal, something she dared not let anyone discover.

If I wanted to hide something, Beatrice wondered, where would I put it? Of course—in my safety deposit box. But if Tony had a safety deposit box the police would already have discovered it and gone through its contents.

I won't give up so easily. Beatrice pressed her slim hands against her temples and saw herself in the mirror. With consternation she leaned forward and pulled out a white hair. Under the huge eyes there was a slight puffiness. Perhaps Mrs George would know something that would get rid of that puffiness or at least cover it. I'm getting old, she thought. Old. And Tony had been young and fresh, triumphant and arrogant in her youth.

Mrs George. The missing paper. Beatrice pulled herself back to the job at hand. For five years this had been her bedroom. If she wanted to hide something, where—

Surely that was the creaking of a floor board. Her heart lurched sickeningly and her hands tightened on the sides of the bench. Her ears strained but there was no other sound. And yet someone was there, near, close at hand. She was aware as she had been that morning of an unseen presence close to her.

It's nerves, she told herself. It's nerves. There's nobody. There was nobody this morning. Was there? This is no time to get rattled.

Eliminate the obvious hiding places. The police must have searched the room; if there was anything here they would have found it. But the police would not know what to look for. They would not know the meaning of that scrap of paper.

Rapidly she went through the dressing table drawers. Tony's tiny desk revealed nothing but unpaid bills. There were no personal letters at all. More and more one wondered about Tony's background. She might have stepped out of a void. There were notices of fashion shows, and a printed announcement of the opening of the Frolic, a new supper club on a roof garden.

Beatrice was about to throw the latter in the waste-basket when her eyes caught a faint penciled line at the bottom. She took it to the light, screwing up her eyes in an effort to decipher the dim writing. 'Don't miss this. Joe.' She looked at it with a frown and then tucked it into her handbag. Probably it meant nothing at all but it was a suggestion, at least, that Tony had acquaintances of whom they had known nothing.

She opened the double doors of the huge wardrobe with its shelves at either end and its line of dresses on padded-satin hangers. It was curious to think that this had once been her own wardrobe.

She began with the drawers, shaking out the delicate underwear, prodding at the rolled hose, exploring the toes of the shoes. Surprisingly, one drawer yielded receipted bills. One did not expect Tony to be careful about keeping records. Certainly, one did not expect her to hoard old laundry lists. Beatrice pushed them to one side and then, being a methodical woman, who overlooked nothing, she picked them up again and looked them over, turning them down one by one.

It was on the back of the fourth one that she found the penciled memoranda. She took it over to the window. A list of directorates, of organizations, in Tony's formless handwriting. Beatrice frowned and saw the scrawled line at the top: 'Miles Aldrich's holdings.' She put the laundry list in her handbag and went back to the rest. There was an envelope with the name of a utility company printed on the front. Beatrice shook it and some newspaper clippings fluttered out on the carpet. They all dealt with the death of Graham Aldrich.

Again a board creaked somewhere but Beatrice, intent on her discovery, was only subconsciously aware of it. What had Graham Aldrich's death to do with Tony? He had died months before she had married Carey. And Miles—had it been Miles who had come downstairs that morning? Why had he lurked out of sight on the terrace? How long had he been there? What was he after?

Miles loved Jennie. Beatrice clung to that for comfort. He wouldn't let her get involved. And Mrs George would keep silent about Jennie's quarrel with Tony if she got back her paper.

Beatrice began on the dresses, taking each one to the light, shaking it, prodding at the shoulder pads. There was a white evening dress she had never seen before and, hanging at the far end of the wardrobe, a new fall suit, the sleeves stuffed with paper. Beatrice pulled the paper from one sleeve and with it a piece of stationery bearing the letterhead of Senator Packard. She glanced at it and put it in her handbag. She wanted to sing, to shout. Eureka! Jennie was safe.

From the other sleeve she pulled a sheet of heavy, expensive stationery. The handwriting was bold and sprawled across the page. The coat of arms was that of Mrs Harrison Ives.

'Correction for page 92, *The Reluctant Lovers*,' it began, and went on in the middle of a sentence:

> ... pulled her down on the couch with a fierce gesture, his mouth cruel, his eyes burning. The weight...

The word 'cruel' had been lined out and over it was written 'sensual.' This in turn had been scratched out and the word 'lascivious' substituted in the margin.

So that, Beatrice thought, is why Mrs Harrison Ives was afraid. And I thought it was Carey she feared. What a fool I am.

She added the paper to the loot in her handbag.

151

Then she pulled up the dressing-table bench and stood on it, examining the hat boxes on the shelves one at a time. There was nothing left but a neat bundle wrapped in brown paper and tied with cord, marked, 'Old clothes to be sent to European relief.' The idea of Tony being moved by the needs of anyone but herself was difficult to swallow, and Beatrice lifted down the package and worked at the knot in the cord. She untied it and opened the brown paper, folding it carefully.

There were a couple of cheap sweaters, a worn skirt, a shabby coat and a sleazy dinner dress. Beatrice looked down at them. These must have been Tony's wardrobe before she married Carey. The contrast between them and the over-crowded closet was staggering.

In the sleeve of the coat she found the hypodermic needle.

*   *   *

'Having fun?'

In her shocked surprise Beatrice dropped the hypodermic on the bed. She could not find her voice.

Carey moved slowly toward her, his eyes searching the open bundle. The change in him struck her like a blow. The boyishness which accounted for so much of his charm was gone. His mouth was tight and thin lipped, his eyes cold. It was impossible to guess what he was thinking.

'Just what are you doing?' There was no friendliness in his tone. He was addressing an impertinent intruder.

Beatrice held out the hypodermic. 'I found this. Tony had hidden it.'

'Well?'

'I don't know,' she admitted. 'I was looking for something that would—' she swallowed— 'tell us something about her past.'

'Do you think it would help to know about my wife's past?'

My wife. With those two words Carey set a barrier between them so vast and insurmountable that Beatrice looked at it aghast. He was treating her like an enemy, wearing his unconcealed hostility like a shield against her.

'I don't know,' she said, and was revolted to realize how abject her voice sounded. 'I found some things. I—'

'Hadn't you better leave that to the police?' Carey watched without comment while she put the hypodermic back in the sleeve of the coat and wrapped the package.

'I'll give this to Lieutenant Mattheson,' she said to the silent man whose eyes followed her movements unwaveringly.

Why doesn't he say something, she wondered. He had moved so quietly she had not even heard him come in. 'Where were you?' she asked.

'In my room. Any objection?'

'I just wondered. I didn't hear you.'

'Perhaps I'd better start wearing a bell around my neck so you'll know where I am. Perhaps I should have done that before.'

'Carey!'

He was deaf to the tortured cry. 'Hadn't you better get the hell out of here?'

'Why, I—' She picked up her handbag and the paper package and preceded him out of the room. He closed the door.

She turned uncertainly into the office, sat down at the desk and tossed off her hat. Her hands were clenched in her lap. She was afraid. But I can't be afraid, she told herself incredulously. Not afraid of Carey.

'What happened this morning?' she asked. 'Did they—bother Jennie much?'

'No.' His tone mocked hers. 'They didn't— bother Jennie much.'

'And Miles?'

'Oh, Miles!' Carey was sardonic. 'No one bothers an Aldrich—much.'

'Why do you hate him so?' She reached for a cigarette and he lighted it for her automatically with one of his swift, graceful movements. Their eyes brushed each other's faces, furtively, questioningly. 'Look, Carey. We mustn't quarrel.'

'Are we quarreling?'

'Let me show you what I found.' She told him about her visit to Mrs George and pulled from her handbag Senator Packard's list, the sheet with Mrs Harrison Ives's corrections, the memorandum of Miles's financial position, the clippings on Graham's death, and the notice of the opening of the Frolic.

Carey looked at them without comment. It was only when he saw the printed announcement of the Frolic opening that he broke his silence. 'What's this? Tony and I went to the opening Monday night but I don't see—'

'Who is Joe?'

'Joe?'

'Yes. See the writing at the bottom.'

Carey glanced at it, frowning. 'That's not Joe. It's T. O. Initials.' He came to lean against the desk beside her. 'Tony insisted on going. There wasn't anything special that I can remember.'

'Did she talk to anyone?'

'I didn't see her speak to a soul. She went off to the powder room once and stayed for fifteen or twenty minutes.'

'Are you sure that's where she went?'

'I didn't follow her.' Carey's tone was dry. 'What are you trying to prove anyhow?'

'I don't know,' Beatrice admitted.

Carey looked down at the loot spread out on the desk. 'So you are going to turn all that over to Lieutenant Mattheson.' His hand reached out and then dropped to his side. 'Everything?'

'No, I'm going to hold on to Senator

Packard's paper for awhile. But first I'll telephone Mrs George to let her know that it is safe.'

'You think of everything, don't you?'

Without reply, she began to gather up her things.

Unexpectedly Carey said, 'You'd better clear out your desk while you are here. I'm going to close the office—for the present, at least.'

'But, Carey, you can't do that!'

'For God's sake,' he said roughly, 'can't you get out? And stay out!'

CHAPTER THIRTEEN

Harland had finished his dinner and was strolling in the little garden in front of his house, a cigarette in his hand. In the dim light he drifted up and down the paths like a shadow made visible only by the crown of white hair and the glowing tip of his cigarette which, like a disciplined firefly, described a half arc each time he lifted it to his lips. He was so deep in thought that now and then he stood stock still, unmindful of his surroundings.

When David and Beatrice arrived almost together, he ushered them into the big book-lined room, switched on lights, and mixed them each a highball. Then he glanced from David's eager face to Beatrice's and broke into a laugh.

'Evidently,' he remarked, 'you two haven't been wasting time. There is news written all over you.'

'Please, teacher,' David begged, 'can I speak my piece first?'

'You had better give him precedence,' Harland advised Beatrice. 'Our reporter has an attack of acute communication coming on and there's no telling what will happen if he is thwarted.' At Beatrice's nod he turned to David. 'Go ahead. Astonish me.'

'Well,' David began, 'at your suggestion I started on the Miles Aldrich angle.'

Harland's eyes twinkled as he watched the eager young red head, but there was affection in his glance. When the youngster had acquired some discipline and perspective he was going to be a first-rate person. It was a pity that the perspective would have to come at the cost of some of his illusions.

David described his search of the newspaper files on Graham Aldrich's death and his conversation with Tim Oleson.

'And after trying to sell me on the idea that Graham must have had his neck broken in the fight at the Club Royale, that Miles didn't have anything to gain by his brother's death and that he had nothing to do with it,' David concluded hotly, 'he gets on the phone to Miles the moment I am out of the place. And he knew Tony. When I said Tony Walker had been

157

killed, he said, "What happened to her?" Anyone would take for granted that Tony was a man's name. Yet he said he didn't know the Walkers.'

There was a brief pause and David said, 'Well, it's important, isn't it?'

'It's interesting,' Harland said cautiously, 'although there isn't the slightest scrap of proof that Tim Oleson ever knew Tony.'

'But there is,' Beatrice exclaimed triumphantly. She cleared the table and emptied the contents of her handbag.

Harland looked from it to her excited face. 'Rather a mixed haul,' he commented. 'You act as though you had the Kohinoor diamond concealed in that mass of rubbish.'

'Don't scoff,' she said. 'Not until you see all of it.'

David, poking at it with a finger, said, 'Laundry lists! What is this anyhow?'

'I've been detecting,' Beatrice explained, 'and I don't know what it means but John is going to tell me.'

The two men laughed.

'He who laughs last,' Beatrice said smugly, and she held out the announcement of the Frolic opening and pointed to the dim line of writing at the bottom with a slim finger. 'I found that in Tony's room this afternoon.'

They bent over, examining it.

'T.O.' David planted a solemn kiss on Beatrice's cheek. 'Don't stop me when I say, "I told you so." Tim Oleson. I've said all along there was a link with Aldrich. Oleson is it.'

'You leap from one conclusion to another like a mountain goat,' Harland complained. He asked Beatrice, 'How did you happen to find this?'

'By accident.' Beatrice explained why she had made the search. 'You see, I thought if Tony was planning to blackmail Mrs George, she might be blackmailing others too. I didn't know what this meant. I just brought it along because it was proof that Tony knew people none of us had heard of.'

'Perhaps Walker knows.'

Beatrice shook her head. 'I showed it to Carey and he never heard of anyone whose initials are T.O. He and Tony went to the Frolic opening Monday evening because Tony insisted. But he didn't see her speak to anyone.'

She spread out the rest of her loot and they went over it in silence. Only the torrid phrases from *The Reluctant Lovers* required an explanation, which David noisily and vehemently refused to credit.

'I take it,' Harland said, 'you've heard of Mrs Harrison Ives.'

'I've heard of the Statue of Liberty too. And it would be easier to think of Liberty laying down the torch and writing the last section of *Ulysses* than to think of Mrs Harrison Ives writing *The Reluctant Lovers*.'

'Concentrate on it,' Harland urged him.

159

'With a little practice, anyone can believe one impossible thing a day.' He leaned back in his chair and fitted his fingertips neatly together. 'And now,' he said, 'I'll tell you how I spent my afternoon.' He checked off the points that he had learned: the partial identification of the man with whom Tony had dined as Alvin, a jilted lover; the fact that she had bought an emerald necklace for cash on Monday afternoon; the fact that she took drugs; the likelihood that her burglar had been the man Alvin, since only the necklace was taken and presumably no one else knew of its existence; and the fact that, whoever had beaten Tony, it was not the burglar.

'I'm getting a little confused,' David admitted.

Harland nodded. 'We've thrown all the pieces of our puzzle in a pile on the table. Let's spread them out and see what we have so far. The questions you have to answer in a murder case are: How? When? Where? Why? Who? We know when and where. We know how—that the radio was deliberately lifted out of its grooves and dropped into the bathtub.'

'It's queer no one heard Tony yell,' David said.

'She probably didn't make a sound. After all, she must have known very well the person who entered her bathroom. It would be simple enough to lean over, as though to move the dial or cut down the volume and pick up the radio.

Dropping it into the water would be a matter of a second or two. Before she had any suspicion of danger, she would be past speech.'

Seeing their somber faces he reached for the glasses. 'May I fix up your drink, Beatrice? David?'

When the glasses were replenished, he resumed, 'Now what do we know about Tony? Her husband has—or at least volunteers— no information beyond, ''Antonia Smith, Chicago.' In six months of marriage, we are to assume, he learned nothing about his wife's family or her friends or her occupation or her income. Perhaps that is true, but it is highly unlikely.'

'Why should Carey lie?' Beatrice protested.

Harland shrugged angular shoulders. 'A marriage that could maintain such a state of uncommunicativeness, of lack of mutual confidences, would be almost unique. And if it actually existed, it would be a powerful indication that Carey and his young wife were not, as he claims, so enraptured with each other that they had no thought for the past; it would indicate that, from the very beginning, they had been a singularly disunited couple. Otherwise, at some stage in their courtship Tony would have revealed something about herself. Love causes a release of confidences; it leads people to talk about themselves. If no such state of confidence existed *at any time*, that marriage begins to look very odd, particularly in the light of the beating that someone administered to Tony.'

'You forget—' Beatrice intervened.

'I wasn't accusing him of murder,' Harland said mildly. 'I was simply pointing to the strange dearth of information he provides about his wife. And there is one thing indicating that he did not know much about her. On Monday she bought an emerald necklace. She wore it on Tuesday evening to dine at an obscure restaurant. But on the evening of the day she got it she went to the gala opening of a supper club and she did not wear it. Why?'

David nodded. 'She didn't want Carey to know she had it. She wouldn't have told him except that it was stolen and she had to get it back.' His forehead puckered. 'Only I don't get it. What good was the necklace if she was going to keep it out of sight? What was she up to?'

Harland opened his hands and brought them together again with a little slap. 'Evidence as to the kind of woman Tony was is beginning to pile up. I think we are safe in assuming that she was a blackmailer. A necklace bought for cash is certainly suggestive. But let's stick to our facts before we start theorizing.

'We know that on Monday Tony bought an emerald necklace for which she paid cash. (Witness—the jeweler who sold the necklace.) We know that Monday night she and Carey

162

went to the opening of the Frolic. Tony apparently went at the suggestion of one T.O. who may or may not be Tim Oleson. (Witness—Carey. Evidence—the printed announcement with its penciled note.)

'We know that on Tuesday evening she dined with a man she called Alvin. (Witnesses—Mrs Jacobs and the waiter.) We know from the same two witnesses that Tony was wearing the emerald necklace and that she paid for the dinner.

'We know that late Tuesday night she called the police to report that the necklace had been stolen by a burglar who had broken into the apartment. Neither the policeman nor her husband believed the story. And,' Harland added slowly, 'Carey behaved as though he had never heard of an emerald necklace. In any case, there is no trace of it so far. We are forced to assume either that her unsavory companion took the necklace or that later she admitted someone else to her apartment.'

He took a long breath. 'Between Tuesday night and Wednesday morning, *after* the burglar had left, someone gave Tony a terrible beating. We know that because the autopsy shows she received those bruises thirty-six to forty-eight hours before her death, and we also have Mrs George's evidence that Tony went to her salon on Thursday morning to try to get them covered up for the cocktail party that afternoon. But why did Tony shield the person

163

who inflicted the beating? If it was Carey—and certainly he is the logical suspect—it would have been more characteristic for Tony at least to hint at the truth.'

Harland broke off. He recalled Tony's impish grin, her laughing comment, 'I've been telling everyone that Carey doesn't beat me. But if anything happened to me now it would be mighty suspicious.' And the pulse hammering in Carey's temple.

He recovered and went on quickly, 'We know that while Tony was at the beauty salon she took advantage of Mrs George's absence to rifle her desk and steal a paper, presumably for the sake of blackmail. Mrs George is our witness that it was stolen while Tony was on the premises and Beatrice has proof that Tony brought the paper home with her.

'Now we come to the cocktail party yesterday afternoon. We know from our separate observations, that Tony was reckless to the point of madness. She was asking for trouble. With the evidence we now have, it is easy to see that she had both Mrs George and Mrs Harrison Ives terrorized. It's my own belief that Mrs George would be more likely to jump through a hoop for her than Mrs Harrison Ives. Mrs George is also an adventuress in her own way and she'd yield to circumstances. She'd cut her losses without too much fuss. But Mrs Harrison Ives doesn't know how to yield. She's one of those all-or-nothing women. She was obviously there under compulsion and she hated it. And,' he added, 'she was afraid.'

Harland glanced from one still face to the other, giving no sign that he was aware of their hostility. 'Then,' he said, 'we come to the unlovely moment when Tony cut Miles out from the pack and kept him with her until the party broke up, so he could not even be found for the announcement of his engagement to Jennie Walker. And after that we have two outbursts of jealous fury: one from Carey, one from Jennie.'

'We always,' David pointed out, a note of desperation in his young voice, 'seem to come back to Miles.'

Harland smiled faintly. 'We always come back to Miles,' he agreed. 'And to me that is the strangest element in the whole business.'

'But—' David began.

'Strange,' Harland went on, without paying attention to the interruption, 'because we know a lot about Miles. His life is lived on the front pages of the newspapers and all the accounts—public and private—agree about him. Lieutenant Mattheson summed it up: Sir Galahad out of Carrie Nation. A narrow, earnest, humorless man, doggedly striving to compensate for the unsavory reputation his father left by devoting himself to good works. And yet you are both assuming—everyone assumed—that this man, who disapproved violently of his brother's loose life, and who was genuinely devoted to Jennie, would lose his head at first sight over a girl as obvious as Tony and make a public display of his weakness on the very day of his engagement. Personally I don't believe a word of it.'

'But,' Beatrice said in bewilderment, 'you can't ignore facts. Miles *did* go off with Tony; he *did* stay away so long Carey couldn't make the announcement. And he came back smeared with Tony's lipstick.'

'And all this,' Harland said gently, 'was because he lost his head over Tony? You think Miles was the aggressor?'

'Then,' David said after a long pause, 'she must have been blackmailing Miles too.'

*   *   *

'And so,' Harland said, 'we come to this morning.' He glanced at Beatrice, who was lying back in her chair, eyes closed. The rouge stood out on her bloodless face and her mouth seemed almost sunken. 'You've had more than you can cope with today. When I get riding my hobby I'm inconsiderate. Let me get you a cab and go home to bed. David and I will carry on awhile longer.'

'No,' she said without opening her eyes, 'I wouldn't sleep yet anyhow. And I don't want to be alone.'

For a moment he studied the haggard face in

concern and then he went on.

'This morning Tony went in to take her bath, turning on her radio about ten-thirty. Carey and Beatrice were both in the office when they heard the radio switch on. Then Carey left for an appointment with Mrs George, who testifies that he was with her. At that time there was no one in the apartment but Tony and Beatrice who were on the lower floor, and the maid Freda and the cook upstairs.

'Shortly after Carey left, Miles Aldrich called to see him and was told that Carey had gone out. Now here we aren't sure of our facts. We know that the door was unlatched. Did Miles leave and return later, during the interval when the door was open, or did he decide to wait for Carey to return? Did someone else enter the apartment while the door was unlatched? The police are making a routine check of the tenants to find out whether anyone was seen in the halls or lobby or elevator but there's little hope they'll turn anything up that way. With an automatic elevator and no doorman, anyone could have gone up unseen.

'During the interval between the arrival of Miles, and Beatrice's discovery of the body, someone came down the stairs and went to Tony's room. Beatrice heard voices raised in argument, thought Tony was abusing the maid, and later heard someone go up the stairs. We know now that it was not Freda. Is that correct, Beatrice?'

'I'm not sure,' she said miserably. 'I heard someone come down, but I'm not sure about the voices. At first I thought it was a soap opera. She loved them. Then I thought I recognized Tony's voice. All I could swear to was that someone came down and went up again.'

'And then,' Harland concluded, 'Beatrice felt that someone was looking at her, grew uneasy, went to Tony's room and found her dead.'

Beatrice was shivering again.

'If Tony was blackmailing Miles,' David said, 'he could have slipped downstairs while Freda was in the kitchen.'

'Anyone might have come downstairs,' Harland said wearily. 'But I boggle at the picture of Miles striding into a woman's bathroom. Not Miles. It takes more imagination than I possess. I can imagine him being stirred by righteous indignation but I don't see him taking bold risks. Particularly when Freda had informed him that Beatrice was downstairs and he must have realized that, in this heat, the office door would be open.'

'But someone took that risk,' David pointed out.

Harland leaned over and picked up the hypodermic. He turned it over and over in his fingers. 'If I were looking for the person who took the gamble of killing Tony in her own apartment I'd look for someone who was

168

emotionally unbalanced and to whom Tony had become a symbol of defeat, something to be repressed at all costs.'

'You mean Alvin, whoever he is,' Beatrice said, her eyes open at last.

'I'd rest easier tonight,' Harland admitted, 'if I knew where Alvin is. I don't like him being at large.'

'Why?'

'Because the act of murder releases something in an unbalanced person, breaks down restraints and controls. The unthinkable has been accomplished and there is no turning back. Murder is a mental hazard only the first time.'

David scraped back his chair. Embarrassment was mingled with stubbornness on his face. 'I know you think Miles Aldrich is my King Charles's head,' he said, 'only I can't help seeing how easy it would be for Oleson to have taken the elevator upstairs—or even walked up—and what a sweat he was in to call Miles after I got out of there this afternoon. Oleson knows something about this business that links Tony and Miles. Look, Mr Harland, how's this? Why can't we go to the Frolic tonight and nose around and find out whether anyone saw Tony with Oleson on Monday?'

'It's definitely an idea,' Harland agreed. 'How about you, Beatrice?'

She shook her head. 'It wouldn't do for me

169

to be seen at a night club the day Tony is murdered. Anyhow, I'm exhausted.' She pulled herself out of her chair. 'But you'll tell me what you learn, won't you?'

'I'll call you tomorrow. Try not to think about it tonight.' He hesitated for a moment. 'This is a fine thing to say when I want you to rest but—'

He was so perturbed that she turned to him in surprise. 'What's wrong, John?'

'Just a fanciful old woman,' he said lightly. 'That's Harland. I get ideas. The thing is that murderers are uneasy people. They get to wondering about the things they overlooked. The newspapers have made a big play of the fact that you—and only you—were downstairs and—'

'You think I'm in danger.' Her voice was steady.

'It's not impossible. You would be wise to bolt your door tonight. Just as a precaution, you know.'

CHAPTER FOURTEEN

'By the way,' Harland said as the taxi swung into Sixth Avenue and started north, 'we haven't discussed salary. I thought perhaps seventy-five a week and expenses. Of course, I wouldn't require all your time.'

'That sounds swell,' David said, but the gloom did not lift from his anxious face. 'Mr Harland, do you think Alvin is the man we are after?'

'It's early days yet,' Harland said. 'We've had less than twelve hours since the murder was committed.'

They took an elevator to the roof where the Frolic offered its dubious joys. The hat-check girl was a ripe blonde in her late thirties. Probably, Harland thought, an ex-chorus girl, tough and knowledgeable. She'd been around. Her eyes summed up the two men. David she dismissed from her notice after a glance at his baggy hand-me-down suit; Harland, after meeting his clear eyes. Nothing for her here.

As they gave her their hats, David asked casually, 'Do you know Tim Oleson by sight?'

She shrugged plump shoulders. 'Who doesn't?'

'Has he been around tonight?'

She shook her head. 'Not since the opening.'

'Did he meet a woman here that night?'

Her eyes had all the softness of Vermont granite. 'I'm a hat-check girl,' she pointed out. 'I don't get inside. He could have danced on the tables and I wouldn't know.'

'Where's the powder room?'

She looked surprised and then jerked her head in the direction of the end of the hall.

'You could see any woman going in there, couldn't you?'

'Sure,' she said. 'Sure. I have nothing to do but watch the customers.' She took a man's hat and handed him a check. 'Nothing at all to do. No customers pestering me.'

'But did you see—'

'Look,' she said firmly, 'I've got a hat-check concession and I intend to keep it. I check hats. I don't watch the customers. I don't see what they do. I got nothing to say. Period.'

Harland intervened. 'We'd better tell you what it is all about. This is a murder case.'

'Where's your badge?'

'I'm not a policeman.'

She shrugged her shoulders.

'Would you prefer,' Harland asked, 'to talk to the police?' As something flickered in her eyes he pressed his advantage. 'Because if you won't give us the information we are after, we'll have to leave it to the homicide squad.'

She licked her lips. 'How do I know what you're after?' she asked at length.

At Harland's nod, David held out the newspaper clipping. The girl looked at the caption:

BRIDE ELECTROCUTED IN PENTHOUSE

Rapidly she scanned the page, studied the photograph of Tony.

'What we want to know,' Harland said, 'is whether you saw that woman at the opening, and whether, to your knowledge, Oleson had

172

any conversation with her.'

The girl looked up then and met Harland's eyes.

'We won't involve you if there is any way to avoid it,' he promised her.

'What has Oleson to do with her?'

'That,' Harland told her, 'is what we are trying to determine.'

She shook her head. 'Tim Oleson wouldn't give his own mother a break. If I say anything he doesn't like, he'll get me bounced out of here. He's done it to other people. Tim thinks he is a combination of Walter Winchell and the late Alex Woollcott. Whatever goes on, I don't want any part of it.'

'It's us—or the police,' Harland reminded her. He slipped a folded bill into her hand and her expression changed as she saw the denomination. 'The police,' he added, 'won't pay you for your information.'

'All right,' she said unsteadily. 'I saw the girl. I remember her because she hung around outside the powder room like she was waiting for someone. Then Oleson came out and they talked for a few minutes.'

'Did you hear what they said?'

She shook her head. 'Not a word. They were down the hall. But there was no quarrel or anything like that. I heard Oleson laugh a couple of times. That's all I know.'

'We are very grateful to you,' Harland said.

'Yeah. Just remember that Oleson's a

stinker from way back. He could blackball me so I'd never get another concession. And don't think he wouldn't do it.'

Harland smiled at her. 'You'll be all right,' he said firmly and collected their hats.

When they reached the street, David said, 'I told you Oleson was no good.'

'He doesn't sound attractive,' Harland admitted.

'And now we have proof he knew Tony. That's something.'

'Something, yes,' Harland admitted. 'But no evidence that their acquaintance had anything to do with her death. I'd like to have a talk with him tonight. Have you any idea where I could find him?'

David shrugged. 'There are no new openings.'

'Suppose we call on him.'

'Now? It's nearly midnight.'

'Late hours are his business. Coming along?'

'Sure.' David grinned. 'I'd like to see his face when he catches sight of me.'

It was twelve-thirty when they reached the reconverted town house where Oleson lived. David glanced up at the second-floor windows where a narrow streak of light gleamed from between the drawn curtains.

'He's home and he's still up,' he said cheerfully. 'At least we won't disturb him.' He set his finger on the button.

The bell rang shrilly but it did not disturb Tim Oleson who lay half sprawling on one of his deep divans, his head down at an awkward angle between his shoulders, and a stain widening across the upholstery.

His murderer jumped at the sound and dropped the ornate fire tongs on the rug, then bent hastily to pick them up, but not before an ugly red and white mess had discolored the light rug.

The murderer wiped off the handle of the tongs and left them on the floor, glanced swiftly around the room, came back to lift a cigarette butt off the ashtray, to switch off the lights. The bell rang again. Footsteps crossed the room almost noiselessly. The door to the kitchenette swung open, closed with a sighing sound, and then the service door opened and closed.

For a moment the murderer paused in the hallway listening, then ran down the service stairs and paused at the basement door.

In the entrance Harland hesitated, then went out to the street. He looked up at the windows. They were dark.

When he rejoined David he said sharply, 'Get the superintendent.'

'What is worrying you?'

'Oleson knows too much. All evening I've been growing more and more aware that he is the key to this whole business.' Harland's voice was tight, rough with impatience. 'What are you waiting for?'

'Sorry,' David said. He pushed the bell marked superintendent. In a few moments the latter, partly dressed and swearing, opened the door.

'Oleson?' he grumbled. 'I mighta known. When there's any trouble, it's always Oleson. You'd think he was the only tenant in the place and I was his personal servant.'

'We just want to make sure nothing is wrong,' Harland explained, reaching for his billfold. 'Won't keep you a minute.'

'It's against orders,' the superintendent said, and as Harland opened the billfold, he laughed. 'All right,' he capitulated. 'Six months Oleson's lived here and I haven't seen a cent of his money yet. Come along.'

'Careful,' Harland warned as they reached the second floor. 'Don't touch the door knob more than you can help. And look out for the light switch. Use my handkerchief.'

The door swung open, the light flashed on and the three men moved forward slowly. No one spoke. The superintendent crossed himself.

Oleson's pudgy body sprawled on the divan. His eyes were half open. The room was filled with the queer whistling sound that was his breathing. Then, without warning, it stopped and the room was still.

'We were just a couple of minutes too late,' David said.

Harland nodded. 'We scared the murderer away.'

'There wasn't time enough to get far.' David wheeled and started for the door.

'Probably used the service staircase or we'd have seen who it was,' the superintendent said and, following his gesture, David went out into the kitchenette and opened the back door.

'We'll have to call the police,' Harland said. 'In fact there are a lot of calls I want to make without delay.'

'The telephone's over there beside the couch,' the superintendent said. His eyes fell on the fire tongs and the revolting mess beside them on the carpet.

'I don't want to use that telephone,' Harland said. 'There may be fingerprints. When my friend gets back tell him he can reach me at the Walkers'. Do you mind waiting for the police? I'll have them here within a few moments.'

'I'll stay,' the superintendent said. He settled down with his back to the man who sprawled on the divan.

In the kitchenette David opened the back door quietly. For a moment he listened. There was no sound. The stairs were dim, with a single bulb burning on the first-floor landing and one in the basement. Cautiously he started down. When he reached the basement he eased open the door that led to the storerooms, furnace room and the superintendent's apartment. There was a muffled sound. The door into the areaway was closing.

David ran down the hall and pulled at the door knob. It held. He turned it again and then observed the catch. By the time he had opened it the areaway was empty. There was no one on the street. The buildings were dark. And across Fifth Avenue lay Central Park. The murderer had got away without a trace.

* * *

The chimes in the penthouse door rang once, twice, and then Harland heard shuffling footsteps. The door opened and Carey stood blinking at him in surprise. He wore trousers, his bare feet thrust into slippers. His eyes were bloodshot.

'Don't you ever sleep?' he demanded and Harland smelled the whiskey on his breath. Carey did not move out of the doorway.

'I've got to use your telephone,' Harland said, 'at once.'

Still Carey did not move. 'And you come clear up here to use a telephone?'

'There's been another murder. A man named Tim Oleson. It has to be reported.'

Carey stepped aside then. He turned on his heel. 'You'll want the police, I suppose,' he said, sat down beside the telephone and dialed. 'What's that name? Address?' When he put down the telephone he said, his voice blurred, 'Bring me a drink, will you? Rye and water. I need it to sober me up. Fix yourself one, too.' He gripped his head in his hands. 'Man at the police desk seemed to think I was a mass murderer when he got my name.' He shook his head, trying to clear it. 'What goes on?'

'I'll answer your questions later,' Harland said. 'Right now I want to make some telephone calls.'

'Checking alibis,' Carey said. 'Well, I've been here all evening but I can't prove it.' As Harland reached for the telephone he clutched it in both hands. 'No,' he said with drunken stubbornness, 'I'll do it myself. What kind of spot do you think this puts me in?'

He dialed a number and waited. 'Hello … Sure I'm drunk, Trix, but don't hang up. I'm calling for your pal Harland … Yeah. Right at my elbow … He's discovered another corpse … Fellow named Oleson … No, he just wanted to be sure you were tucked up for the night … I'll call you tomorrow.' He set down the telephone. 'Who next?'

While he was speaking, Harland had flipped the pages of the telephone directory. He placed a list in front of Carey who blinked in surprise, looked at Harland to see whether he was serious, and then began to dial.

Mrs Harrison Ives, her maid said, had left orders that she was not to be disturbed until nine in the morning. Mrs George lived at a hotel on Lexington in the fifties. The phone rang and rang. At length Mrs George said breathlessly, 'Yes? What is it?'

An impish expression crossed Carey's face. 'This is the hotel detective,' he said in a rough tone. 'Are you alone?' There was a gasp, a muffled whisper, and he hung up, grinning. 'Include her out,' he told Harland cheerfully. 'She's got company.'

He dialed the next number and waited. A man servant answered. Mr Aldrich was not at home. If Mr Walker would leave a message—

Carey reported to Harland and looked at the last name on the list. 'Damn it,' he exploded savagely, 'do it yourself! I won't hound my own sister.'

Harland made the call. At length he heard Margaret Walker's sleepy voice.

'Mrs Walker, this is John Harland. I'm terribly sorry to call you so late, but something has happened and I am anxious to speak to your daughter.'

'To Jennie?' Margaret sounded bewildered. 'At—quarter of one? What has happened?'

'Something rather unpleasant, I am afraid. Do you mind calling her?'

'But she's not here,' Margaret said. 'She's spending the evening with Carey. She didn't think he should be alone. She hasn't come home.'

CHAPTER FIFTEEN

Only one light burned in the room, a reading lamp which shone on the leather chair, making it seem as red as blood. It lighted Harland's bony hands with their large knuckles, moving rapidly as he shuffled the cards and dealt another game of solitaire. It lighted the white hair and the deep-set eyes that looked somberly at the cards.

There was no sound but the snap of the cards as Harland laid them down. At half-past four in the morning traffic was so light that noises which would pass unnoticed during the day— the occasional rumble of a truck, the headlong rush of a fast car, the voices of late revelers— were loud in the room.

Harland swept up the cards, shuffled the pack, and began to build a cardhouse, setting each card lightly in place with careful, precise gestures. He reached for a cigarette, lighted it, and contemplated the flimsy structure. Then he reached forward, dislodged one card and the others fluttered down on the table.

He got up and began to pace the room slowly, conscious of a faint nausea. I haven't the stomach for this kind of thing, he told himself. It always begins in a scientific spirit and it ends in nausea. What good does it do? I understand now why it happened; I see that the whole monstrous tragedy grew out of the qualities inherent in a group of people; that once the proper circumstances existed, the rest was bound to follow. I know that the seeds of the trouble go back to the intangibles that shaped these characters. And when I know all that—

He kicked a footstool savagely out of his way. What good does it do? He could see that the murder was avenged and that was not enough. The ideal solution was to prevent it in the first place. When would men accumulate enough data to be able to spot the potential murderer and forestall the crime?

A window took shape grayly. Outside a bird stirred uneasily and uttered a faint, sleepy twitter. Harland flung open the door and walked out into the dark garden. The moon was down. The stars were fading. Another day was breaking—and he hated it.

*　　　*　　　*

The butler opened the door, weighed Harland with practiced eyes from the quiet distinction of his bearing to the well-cut clothes, and permitted his expression to change from one of disapproval to one of aloof inquiry.

'Good morning,' Harland said. 'It's preposterously early, I know, but I wanted to catch Mr Aldrich before he leaves the house. Will you tell him Mr Harland is calling and that I would not disturb him at this hour if it could be avoided.'

'I will inquire,' the butler said, 'whether Mr Aldrich is up yet.'

Harland glanced around and strolled into a huge drawing-room, the draperies still drawn at the windows, the furniture shrouded in dust covers for the summer.

The butler hesitated for a moment and then started up the stairs. Harland surveyed the room, its big oil paintings, the ornate Italian furniture, the small gilt chairs. It was tasteless and ostentatious. He pulled back one of the drapes and saw the broad, sun-flooded avenue, the trees in Central Park dusty with summer, a couple cantering along the bridle path, a stream of private cars, taxis, buses.

The butler returned. 'Mr Aldrich's compliments and will you join him for coffee, sir? This way, please.' He led the way up to the second floor and to the back of the house and opened a door on a cheerful, sunny room with chintz covers on the furniture.

Miles was sitting at a small table, his breakfast in front of him, the morning paper still folded beside his plate, while a radio voice related the news of the hour.

He stood up, shook hands, and waved Harland into a chair across from him.

'I owe you an apology,' Harland began.

'Not at all. I am an early riser.' Miles, Harland thought, was the kind of man who

183

makes a virtue of his digestion.

'I've ordered some coffee,' Miles said, 'but won't you join me at breakfast, too?'

'Thank you. I've already breakfasted. But coffee would be nice.'

'I always think,' Miles told him, 'that the early hours of the day are the best. Start the day early, after eight hours of sound sleep; start it properly with a good, sustaining breakfast, and you won't be troubled with stomach ulcers.'

'Someone,' Harland commented, 'said that ulcers are the wound stripes of civilization.'

'That's clever,' Miles agreed. 'No truth in it though. Ulcers are the result of self-indulgence.'

'You believe in prompt reprisals,' Harland commented.

Miles's close-set eyes could be searching. They searched now for a hidden meaning in the casual words.

'I believe,' he said firmly, 'that nature always takes its revenge.'

A maid brought Harland a cup and saucer and Miles filled the cup from a slender silver coffeepot beside his plate. He moved away the newspaper with the air of a man clearing his desk for action.

'And now, Mr Harland,' he began.

Harland reached for the newspaper, opened it, and laid it before Miles. 'That's why I am here,' he said.

184

Miles's eyes followed Harland's pointing finger:

NEWS MAN MURDERED
Tim Oleson, Night-club reporter, Beaten to Death

The body of Tim Oleson, well-known figure in New York's night spots, was found in his apartment at twelve-thirty this morning. He had been beaten over the head with a pair of heavy fire tongs.

The discovery was made by David Morehouse, a reporter and colleague of Oleson's, and John Harland, distinguished author of the best-seller, *Man's Worst Enemy*. When Oleson did not answer their ring, the door was opened by the superintendent.

No motive for the brutal killing is known as there appears to be no evidence that robbery was attempted. A billfold on the body contained over fifty dollars.

Tim Oleson, a prominent figure in New York's night life, began his career as...

Miles skimmed the obituary material rapidly.

Oddly enough, this is the second time within twenty-four hours that the mystery man, John Harland, has been associated with a murder case. Yesterday morning, when the body of the beautiful Mrs Carey Walker was found electrocuted in the bathtub of her duplex penthouse, Mr Harland was present while the police questioned the family...

Miles reread the paragraph, folded the paper neatly, and put it down. All his movements were controlled, quiet. He took his time. At length he looked at Harland.

'A distressing thing,' he said. 'Distressing. But I don't quite—why are you bringing the story to my attention?'

'Because Tim Oleson telephoned you yesterday afternoon and said that it was important.'

Miles patted his neat mustache with a heavy linen napkin. 'There's some mistake. I never heard of the man until this moment.'

'And yet there is no possible mistake about the telephone call,' Harland said gently. 'It was overheard.'

'And perhaps you know why this total stranger called me?' There was a metallic sound in Miles's voice.

Harland was unmoved. 'Perhaps I do.'

'Well?'

'Tim Oleson was, as you may have gathered from the article, a night-club habitué.'

'Anyone who knows me,' Miles began, 'can tell you that night clubs and all they stand for—drinking, debauchery, vice—are anathema to me.'

186

'Tim Oleson,' Harland went on, 'was at the Club Royale the night your brother Graham was—injured.'

Miles pushed back his chair and went to stand at the window looking down on a small, walled garden at the rear of the house. It was a long time before he turned around. He sank into a chair.

'Sometimes it seems as though my brother has caused me more trouble dead than alive. How he would enjoy knowing that! It's true this man Oleson called me yesterday. He said he knew who had killed my brother.'

Harland looked interested but he made no comment. Miles fidgeted. He straightened his impeccable necktie; touched the handkerchief carefully folded in his breast pocket, smoothed the neat mustache and his thinning hair.

'I've never even seen Oleson. I don't know anything about him. I didn't kill him. It's true he called me up yesterday, but I told him I wasn't interested. Do you hear that? I wasn't interested.'

'That was rather an extraordinary attitude.'

'I can't expect you to understand,' Miles said, 'the way I felt about Graham. People get ridiculous ideas about the wealthy. If you have money they think you are pampered, idle, useless. As far back as I can remember,' he got to his feet and looked down at Harland from burning eyes, 'as far back as I can remember, I was brought up to be a sober, God-fearing

Christian. My father felt his own mistakes and he wanted to make public restitution through his sons. We were his instruments.'

And there, Harland thought, you never spoke a truer word.

'All through my childhood,' Miles went on, 'I was trained for one thing: to bring good into the world, to eradicate evil. When I was only seven, I began dividing my pocket money with poor boys. From the day I entered college I looked around for causes that were worthy of my time and the money my father was already beginning to entrust to me. To my mind that money has always been a trust, dedicated to the Lord's service.'

The pupils in the close-set eyes were wide as though he looked on darkness; the metallic voice was falling into a rhythmic chant; the man swayed as he stood before Harland.

'And at every turn,' he said, 'something has stood in my way, as though the devil himself stood between me and the good I wanted to do.'

Harland felt a shiver run along his spine as the voice grew higher, the strange, primitive rhythm more marked.

'Do you know something, Harland? God punishes those He loves. He tests them. Whatever I did, whatever I've done, something spoiled it. When I gave my allowance to the slum children, they laughed at me, but they played with Graham who would not have given them a penny. I didn't make friends in college though I was a conscientious student, but Graham was kicked out of three schools and he was popular with everyone.

'All these years I've been trying to live as my father would have wanted me to live, but the newspapers would give a paragraph to me when I took children to a summer camp and a column to Graham when he was sued for breach of promise. He was rotten, rotten clear through.' Miles was shaking and he grasped the back of the chair to steady himself.

'It was God's judgment,' he said in a quieter tone, 'that Graham should be killed in a drunken brawl in a night club. As a man lives, so shall he die.'

Harland filled a glass with water and brought it to him. 'Sit down,' he said, his voice authoritative but emotionless. 'Don't talk any more until you drink this.'

Miles obeyed him and gradually the trembling stopped and the tension faded from his face.

'You didn't like Graham,' Harland said then. 'You were glad when he died.' As Miles's lips parted, he put up his hand. 'You regarded it as a just punishment. And you know nothing of Tim Oleson who called you a few hours before his own murder. Do you mind telling me where you were between twelve and one this morning?'

'I went for a walk,' Miles said.

'Do you usually walk at that time of night?'

'No.'

'Did you see anyone you knew?'

'I walked in the park. I couldn't sleep. The death of Mrs Walker had been a great shock—'

'You were at the penthouse at the time she died, I remember. Why,' Harland asked, 'were you so reluctant to make your presence known?'

'I came to see Carey.' Miles pulled out a handkerchief and patted his forehead. The hysteria had dropped away, leaving a colorless, meticulous man. 'As he was the head of my fiancée's family, I felt that I owed him some explanation for my behavior at his cocktail party. When I learned that he was out I decided to wait for him.'

'It might help to clear the way if you would tell me what happened,' Harland said. 'I am not asking out of curiosity. I will not repeat anything you say unless it throws light on these two murders. I am aware, of course, that Miss Jennie was mistaken about your interest in Mrs Walker, who was not the type of woman to attract you.'

'Quite mistaken,' Miles agreed, proud of this faith in his lack of human weakness. 'Mrs Walker had something of importance to say to me. She told me that she knew my brother Graham had been murdered and she knew who had killed him. The—kisses were—just an impulse on her part.'

'And as a result of what Tony said, you came to see Carey.' Harland's eyes were half closed. 'Freda told you Carey was out. There was a disturbance in the kitchen and she left you alone. You waited in the living-room with the outside door ajar.' Harland's eyes were as clear as mirrors. 'Then the elevator stopped and someone got out. Someone you were not prepared to see at the moment. You went to the terrace, and the person—whoever it was— walked downstairs. Shall I tell you who that person was, Mr Aldrich?'

'It was Jennie, of course,' Miles said, like a spent runner. 'I'd never guessed what she was like until the party. She seemed—good. Not ambitious like Carey. Not frivolous like her mother. A fine, noble woman with sound principles. I had planned such a beautiful life for the two of us.' His manner demanded Harland's pity. 'Such a splendid, useful life. And then I saw her face ugly with rage and her voice screaming and all the hate in her. She didn't believe in me. It's a terrible thing, Mr Harland, to know that I must go down my appointed path without a helpmate. Alone.' There was a tremolo in his voice like that of a badly trained soprano.

Harland got to his feet. 'Yes,' he said, 'it must be. Thanks for seeing me.' He left so swiftly that Miles blinked after him in surprise.

CHAPTER SIXTEEN

Mrs Harrison Ives was a happy woman. If she had not been so stately she would have seemed downright exuberant. She brushed aside Harland's apologies as casually as she brushed aside the manuscript on which she was at work. A morning visit, she declared, was delightful. When dear Mama had been alive and she was a mere child they had frequently paid morning visits. It was early, but a glass of sherry, perhaps?

A glass of sherry, by all means, Harland agreed, and watched Mrs Harrison Ives, wearing a dowdy dress of nondescript brown, positively prance about the room as she set out a decanter and glasses and rang for biscuits. And all the time she could barely restrain herself from bursting into song.

'There are so many questions I want to ask you,' she said, and although she sat down cautiously, her weight made Harland bounce at the other end of the couch. 'So many things that occurred to me while I was reading your splendid book. So inspiring.'

Harland smiled at her and raised his glass.

'You look,' Mrs Harrison Ives said bluntly, 'as though you hadn't slept a wink.'

'I haven't,' Harland admitted.

'You must let me give you my prescription. I

192

took only one pill last night and yet I slept ten hours, like a baby.'

'I noticed when I came in,' he said truthfully, 'that you look like a woman who has shed all her worries.'

The couch protested as Mrs Harrison Ives shifted her position. 'You are up to something,' she said. She had steady eyes and her broad hands had strength and determination.

'I've come,' he protested, 'simply to continue our conversation about psychology.'

She nodded. 'You take little pieces and fit them together. Yes, I remember.'

Certainly there was no hysteria about Mrs Harrison Ives. She folded her hands on her ample lap and waited.

'The process isn't entirely my own,' Harland said. 'Lots of people do it. And sometimes— they get the wrong picture.'

'What kind of picture?'

Harland's hands were cupped, shaping imaginary pieces. 'This one is an odd-shaped piece, a girl from nowhere. She's an active girl and rather like a magpie in some respects. She—collects things. Sheets of paper containing—shall we say—feverish prose. And she buys an emerald necklace for cash.' He paused and the woman beside him did not stir, her basilisk gaze did not waver.

'And here,' he made another gesture, 'is a second piece, a woman who writes feverish prose, a woman who remains in New York

193

during the heat of the summer for the first time in her life, a woman whose bank account, I think, has been depleted of fifteen thousand dollars which she withdrew in cash.'

Mrs Harrison Ives did not move.

Harland looked down at his imaginary picture and made a movement as though fitting the two pieces together; the impact of his eyes was almost a shock. 'And then,' he said briskly, 'the first piece—' and he made a gesture which swept it off the table. 'Murder. It's like a one-celled animal. It reproduces itself. Splits off. Early this morning there was a second murder, a man named Tim Oleson.'

'I saw the story in the *Herald-Tribune*,' Mrs Harrison Ives said. 'I'd never heard of him before.'

'We tried to reach you last night by telephone. Your maid said you could not be disturbed.'

'I went to bed. I took a sleeping pill.'

Harland finished his sherry. 'Our call was made between twelve-thirty and quarter of one. It would be a wise precaution to mention to your maid that you were awake and heard the bell.' He smiled suddenly. 'Ten hours is too much sleep anyhow.'

*   *   *

Lexington Avenue was noisy with truck drivers who proceeded on the simple theory, uncorrected by experience, that constant horn-blowing would speed up a stalled motor. The sidewalks were filled with people who, regardless of the heat, plunged ahead, like the man in *Alice in Wonderland* whose time was worth a thousand pounds a minute.

To Harland, the eternal spectator, there was something monstrous in the relentless haste of people, most of whom were obviously going nowhere at all; frightened, harassed, tenaciously hopeful people plunging ahead of a speeding taxi, beating a traffic light, squeezing onto an overcrowded bus to save a minute.

Stop, he wanted to tell them; minutes weren't given you to save but to spend. This is yours—now. Stop and live it.

The Budget Hat Shop—all One Price—Margaret Walker, Prop.—was almost empty. A salesgirl, with a harassed expression and a fixed smile, was trying a hat on an oversized matron who expected to be transformed into Ingrid Bergman for $2.35 plus sales tax.

Harland found Margaret putting hats back on their stands. Her piquant face lighted up and she held out her hand. 'Mr Harland! How nice.' She had, he thought, a special talent for making one feel welcome.

'I hope I'm not in the way.'

'Not at all. We aren't busy today.' She moved a chair for him and sat down like a woman of infinite leisure.

'Couldn't you turn this place over to your

clerks and lunch with me?' he asked. 'My housekeeper will give you fresh cold salmon on crisp lettuce leaves and tiny crescent rolls and perfect coffee.'

'Get thee behind me,' she muttered. 'There's such a thing as cruel and inhuman punishment.'

'Why not?'

'Bertha's out with a cold and after twelve o'clock business picks up. Saturday afternoon is always busy. And Pearl means well but she hasn't any real flair for salesmanship.'

'Let them go hatless then,' he said with the ease of a man who has a regular income.

The mischievous smile crossed Margaret's face. 'I have no right to do it but I will, just the same. Give me a minute to clean up.'

Actually, it wasn't more than five minutes before she returned, and he gave her full marks. As they passed the customer, Margaret said, 'Just a minute,' turned, looked at the woman with her head a little on one side and then picked up a hat, murmured, 'What madam needs is this line, Pearl,' and adjusted the hat carefully.

'That,' the customer said in an unexpectedly soft voice, 'is just what I have been looking for.'

Margaret nodded, smiled, and went out onto the hot street. A cab stopped, Harland helped her in and gave his address.

He felt a little nervous as he unlocked the

door in the wall and led her through his garden, as though it would be a disaster if she did not like his house. He watched Mrs Larsen tensely when she put the luncheon before them, worried for fear something should go wrong.

But Margaret liked his garden and his house and his food. She kept up a flood of light, casual chatter until the iced coffee was set before them and it seemed to Harland that he had never before appreciated his own house or sufficiently praised his housekeeper. He discovered, with surprise and wry amusement, that he was working hard to entertain Margaret Walker, to bring laughter into her eyes. He was deliberately showing off and it made him feel foolish, unexpectedly young, and exhilarated.

The exhilaration died, however, when she went to look out of the window and the light fell on her face, making her look worn and old. She had slept little and there was a nervous tremor about her mouth. Harland felt a stab of pity and dropped his inconsequential chatter.

'Now, then,' he said quietly, 'let's talk about it. You've got it all bottled up inside, and unless you let off steam something is going to crack.'

'I know,' she admitted, 'but there isn't anyone to talk to. I simply can't say anything to Carey or Jennie. They have enough to bear. And after working so many years, I find I have almost no close women friends. Just men who take me to dinner and the theater.' She considered. 'It's ridiculous at my age, isn't it? No wonder Miles does not approve of me.'

Harland laughed. 'I can picture you at ninety, riding out in a wheelchair, with a couple of aged gallants tottering along and quarreling as to which one shall push you.'

'At ninety?' she retorted. 'Nonsense. I'll be navigating under my own steam.' The smile faded. 'It's hardly decent,' she said, 'to be joking when only twenty-four hours ago Tony was killed. And so young. So young.'

'Were you fond of her?' Harland asked.

'No,' she admitted candidly, 'I didn't really like her. But it may not have been Tony's fault. I didn't like my son's first wife either. Perhaps I am just a bad mother-in-law.'

'Why didn't you like them?'

'Because,' Margaret said, 'they wanted so much. It doesn't make for happiness. But in a way the fact that I didn't like Tony makes me feel worse about her death. Can you understand that?'

'Yes,' he assured her, 'I understand that. Her death was an ugly business but it's over for her. The evil that men do lives after them. It isn't over for the people Tony hurt. It's just beginning.'

Margaret, in some subtle fashion, had withdrawn from him. She was still smiling, still friendly, but remote, out of reach, barricaded against him.

'All the way to your shop,' he said, 'I found

myself filled with romantic notions I thought had ended when I was twenty. About carrying you off somewhere out of all this ugliness. Where it couldn't hurt you.'

'And where,' Margaret said with a crooked smile, 'do you think that would be?'

'I told you they were romantic notions. Then it occurred to me that you'd be wondering and worrying and no one has really told you what was going on. I always think,' he added cheerfully, 'that it's easier to know. Don't you?'

'Oh, yes, indeed,' Margaret said, and looked fixedly out of the window.

Harland told her then what they had learned about Tony, about the drugs, the blackmailing, and the burglar.

'Do you think they will find him?'

'They've almost had their hands on him twice: once when he tried to pawn the necklace, once when he tried to give it to a druggist for some dope. He got away both times but he seems to leave a wide trail. Anyhow, if he doesn't show up soon, we'll smoke him out.'

Margaret took a long breath. 'Do you think he killed her?'

'That's a problem for the police,' he answered evasively.

'Carey's—brooding,' she said and he knew she had started to say something else.

'He's drinking heavily,' he told her. 'My dear, you must realize that it is obvious to anyone who sees him.'

'It's been getting worse,' she said. 'Worse and worse.' She blinked tears out of her eyes and said almost angrily, 'Those two children of mine—they're so wretchedly unhappy.'

Harland lifted his arms and let them drop helplessly. 'And yet now and then,' he said in a tone of wonder, 'I actually regret having no wife and children. I must be demented.'

'The worst thing,' Margaret said fiercely, 'is being helpless. Seeing them suffer and knowing that you can't help.'

'I suspect you help more than you know.' As she shook her head he insisted, 'You keep them on an even keel.'

'I?' Margaret was incredulous. 'My dear man, I'm a preposterous mother.'

His smile was warm and reassuring. 'You're there,' he said. 'A sphere of quiet and peace for them to come to when they need you. And you have something else to give those two serious children of yours—lightness of heart.'

'Another word,' she warned him unsteadily, 'and I shall probably burst into tears.'

'How long since you have?'

'I don't know. Years.'

'Don't try to be too strong,' he said gently. 'The burden is not so heavy if you shift it now and then.'

'There are times,' Margaret told him, 'when I want to sit down and tear my hair and scream. I'm too old to adjust myself to all these
200

situations. When I was a girl no woman ever went to a party where her son's two wives were hostesses. It may be all right but it is too much like being one of those Oriental potentates or something.'

'Awkward, of course, but what could you do?'

'I'm a practical woman. Not clever but practical. When something is wrong I want to straighten it out. And here is Carey trying to drink himself to death. And poor Jennie—'

Harland examined her, his white head cocked on one side. 'I must say,' he commented, 'you don't look practical. It's an awfully bread-and-butter sort of word. It doesn't suit you in the least.'

Margaret laughed and abruptly the laughter died.

'What is it?' Harland asked.

'Why did you ask me to lunch?' she said. 'Is it Jennie?' Her hand reached out, clutched at his sleeve. 'Nobody could do anything to Jennie, could they?'

'Do what to her?'

'You aren't telling me anything! Why did you try to get her on the telephone so late last night?'

'Because,' Harland said evenly, 'Carey refused to do it.'

'Carey! But she was with Carey—she—'

'Last night Tim Oleson was murdered.'

Margaret's face was blank with bewilderment.

Harland repeated David's story about
Oleson witnessing Graham Aldrich's death
and his attempt to reach Miles. Then, softening
the details, he described the finding of Oleson's
body.

'The police were on the job all night. There
are no fingerprints, no known motives. So far,
David and I haven't told Lieutenant
Mattheson about Oleson's link with Tony but
it must be done without delay.'

There was anguish in Margaret's face. 'Then
you think—what do you think?'

'I think Tony lived by blackmail and that she
in turn was being blackmailed by Oleson.'

Margaret frowned. 'I could understand
better if she had killed him, but she died first.
And what has all this to do with Jennie?'

'Let's ask her and see,' Harland suggested
sensibly.

CHAPTER SEVENTEEN

The tall girl with the round shoulders and
spotty complexion talked out of the side of her
mouth to a dumpy girl with a round, vacant
face and stupid eyes. There was no necessity for
talking out of the side of her mouth; no one was
near enough to overhear the conversation; but

that was the way girls learned to exchange confidences in the institution from which she had just been released.

'Walker's on a rampage,' she said.

'Yeah?' The dumpy girl was mildly surprised.

'She made Stella clean her face and what she didn't say about girls who wear too much make-up and what happens to loose women. Stella's in the John crying her eyes out.'

'She would be,' the dumpy girl agreed. 'She had a kind of a crush on Walker. I never knew the old girl to blow off before. Sometimes I wish she would. Better than preach—preach—preach all the time. And "Bring me your little troubles, girls." I wonder,' the dumpy girl said from the vast experience of fifteen, 'what she'll do if she ever hears the facts of life.'

'She won't,' the tall girl said. 'Some day she's going to clap her hands and say, "Now, girls, today we're going to have a lovely, lovely time. We are all going to look under rose bushes for babies."'

The fat girl snorted and the tall one, with so appreciative an audience, warmed to her task. 'And the one who finds the most,' she went on in a tone of ecstasy, 'will win a lovely, lovely prize. A free ticket to hear a lecture on the old-fashioned girl—and was she a dope.'

As a tinny piano began to beat out 'The Blue Danube Waltz' with remorseless precision, the two girls ran into a big barren room to join a cluster of a dozen other girls who were forming into double lines.

Pathetic attempts had been made to transfer the loft floor of an abandoned building into a social hall. Bunting had been tacked on the walls along with sentimental, highly colored magazine covers and mottoes of an inspirational nature. But the decorations had not caught an authentic note of gaiety. They drooped in a disheartened manner.

In front of the girls stood Jennie Walker, looking much more attractive in a gym suit than in her usual clothes. It revealed the largely built but well-proportioned body, the firm proud lines of her breasts, the flat stomach, the good legs with their slim ankles. Compared to the poor complexions of the girls her own glowed with health.

She waited ostentatiously until the two latecomers had taken their places and then clapped her hands. At her signal the music stopped.

'Now, girls,' Jennie began, and she sent a beaming smile of good will along the two straggling rows. Sometimes, she thought, it was really discouraging. If just once they would smile back, respond to the friendship she offered them so freely. But they stood there, apathetic, unresponsive.

Jennie's smile broadened, her voice grew even brisker as she announced the lovely, lovely surprise for the week. Next Saturday she was going to take them all to the Cloisters and they were going to have a treat, an outdoor supper that had been paid for by a dear friend of hers who was so interested in them. 'You know, I've told him all about you and what dear girls you are.'

'Walker's got a boy friend,' one of the girls whispered to another.

This was the treat that Miles had suggested before All Was Over. The last time he would ever share her confidences, her anxiety about them, and offer to help.

Jennie flashed a quick look up and down the lines but there was no animation, no response. The girl from the reformatory gave her an ironic glance that Jennie failed to understand. Stella had washed her face and now she looked like any girl; she had lost that queer, unsettling resemblance she bore now and then to Tony.

The smile faded from Jennie's face. Why don't they like me, she wondered. Why? I try so hard. I want to help them. And down inside they're laughing at me.

She stood erect, raised her arms shoulder high, and nodded to the pianist. Once more the piano beat out its tinny version of 'The Blue Danube Waltz' and Jennie, lowering her arms, raising them, chanted, '*One*, two, three. *One*, two, three.'

Without turning, she knew by the expression of heightened interest on the girls' faces that someone had entered the room behind her. She threw more vigor, more determined gaiety into her voice.

When the pianist had finished with two loud chords, Jennie said, 'And now let's gather around the piano, girls, and sing together. I always think nothing brings people closer together than singing.'

Someone snickered but Jennie went on bravely, 'A lovely old English song, "Who is Sylvia?"'

She stepped back and half turned, casting a quick glance at the man who stood waiting. The smile died away completely. She walked toward him, her step heavy.

'Yes?'

'My name is John Harland,' he said. 'You probably don't remember me.'

There was something familiar about the thin figure, the narrow face and white hair. She had seen him—she groped in her memory—out of doors somewhere. Oh, on Carey's terrace. He had been there when she told Tony she wished she was dead. He had been there when Tony's body had been carried up the stairs and taken away.

'Yes?' she said again, but he knew that she remembered. She looked sick.

The pianist tapped her foot loudly and fourteen voices, in what appeared to be fourteen keys, demanded to know the identity of Sylvia.

'Your mother told me where to find you,'

206

Harland said. 'I kidnaped her from the shop and made her lunch with me.'

He neither looked nor acted like a policeman and he wore the fatuous expression men got when they spoke about her mother. And yet her mother was fifty-five and didn't even try to conceal it. She was always boasting about her grown-up children and she never said, 'Of course, I married when I was a mere child.' And it wasn't, Jennie thought resentfully, that her mother was a raving beauty. Why, she was old! And yet three times out of four when the telephone rang it wasn't for Jennie who was only twenty-five. It was for her mother. It wasn't right; it wasn't fair.

'Yes?' she said for the third time.

'This is all new to me,' Harland said, watching her changing expression. 'May I look on? It seems to be a very—ah—useful work.'

Jennie's eyes brightened. 'Of course you can. You know our organization deals with poor, underprivileged girls who have—been misguided and got on the wrong path. We are showing them that they can have a second chance. Give them really homey surroundings and a chance to discover the Finer Things of Life.' Her voice rose, trying to carry above the voices that asked shrilly, 'Is she kind as she is fair?'

Harland nodded and sat down on a bench against the wall while Jennie hurried to the piano, slipped her arm around the waist of a

207

tall girl with bad skin, and joined in the singing. And lo, Harland thought, poor Jennie's voice led all the rest. He observed that the girl beside her looked up in surprise at the unexpected embrace and then gave Harland a cynical glance.

What in heaven's name, he wondered, brought Jennie with her really incredible innocence among these waifs, all of whom knew more about their world than she would ever guess.

The singing was followed by some robust folk-dancing and then Jennie clapped her hands.

'That's all for today, girls! And remember our lovely, lovely treat for next Saturday. And don't forget,' her voice lowered, became embarrassingly intimate, 'whenever you want to come to me for advice, you have my telephone number. And we can have a lovely little chat.'

'Thank you, Miss Walker,' the girls chorused and then ran toward the dressing room.

For a moment Jennie looked after them. They wouldn't call, of course. They never did. And yet she truly, truly wanted to help them.

When she had paid the pianist and dismissed her, Harland said, 'What rewarding work you are doing.'

'Oh, yes,' Jennie said brightly. 'Oh, yes.'

'Can we talk here?'

'If you like.'

Harland's face was grave now and filled with a kind of pity. 'I wish,' he said abruptly and with a sincerity that took her by surprise, 'that I didn't have to come to you with this ugly story, but it has to be done. And anyhow,' a smile began in his eyes and warmed them before it reached his lips, 'if I didn't do it, I'd have David Morehouse at my throat.' He summed her up and said the one perfect thing. 'It's rare to find a knight in armor charging around in this modern world.'

'That's an odd way to describe David,' Jennie said, groping her way to a new idea. 'He takes nothing seriously.'

'He takes you seriously. He lost his job so he could be on hand when your sister-in-law died, and he's working for me now, so we can help clean up the whole horrible business.'

Jennie's face was transformed; it held the wonder and delight of a child's eyes seeing their first lighted Christmas tree. 'David did that?'

Harland nodded. 'However, I didn't come here to plead his cause like something out of "The Courtship of Miles Standish." I came because we've got a lot of things to clear up and I hoped it would be easier for you to have me do it than the police.'

'I don't see,' Jennie said, 'why the police should want to talk to me. I don't—there isn't anything—just because—'

'Someone,' Harland said quietly, 'murdered

your sister-in-law by electrocuting her. Tony got in someone's way and Tony was removed. And the murderer thinks, "How easy it is!" And another person gets in the way. So the murderer strikes again. After that, murder could easily become a kind of habit. For the murderer feels, "I want this; therefore, I have a right to it." But the murderer is not a fool, not stupid enough to believe that the motive for murder can be concealed. And so—'

'You sound,' Jennie said through numb lips, 'as though you know who the murderer is.'

'Yes,' Harland told her sadly. 'I know.'

There was a long pause and she said, 'Go on.'

'And so the murderer behaves like the people in the sleigh who threw their babies to the wolves to enable them to get away.'

'But how?'

'Let me give you an example,' Harland said. Jennie tried to look away from his eyes but they held her inexorably. 'Let's suppose that there is a young woman who wants things to be pleasant for the people she loves. She has an older brother to whom she is devoted. Unexpectedly, the brother's first marriage is broken and he brings home a young wife. The sister discovers that the second wife is a bad influence on her brother, that he is unhappy, that he is becoming a chronic drunkard. And the young wife proves to be a girl without fine feelings or understanding, one who hurts the sister whenever she can.

'Then the sister becomes engaged to be married, and the young wife snatches away her fiancé at the very party at which the engagement is to be announced. The sister, righteously indignant but indiscreet, has a public quarrel with her, and a few hours later the young wife is dead, out of the way, no longer a threat either to a beloved brother's happiness or her own. And the sister is unable or unwilling to account for her actions at the time of the murder.

'Twelve hours later, a man named Tim Oleson is beaten over the head and dies so that he can never reveal the thing he knew about the dead wife. And when the sister is called, to make sure that she has an alibi for this second murder, she is supposed to be with her brother. And that is false.'

'But,' Jennie looked at him in mounting horror, 'but—I never even heard of this Tim Whatshisname.'

'But it's a pretty good baby to throw to the wolves,' Harland suggested.

'Yes, I can see that,' Jennie admitted honestly. 'But anyone who knows me could tell you I wouldn't hurt anyone. I couldn't possibly kill anyone.'

'But you aren't awfully truthful, are you?'

Jennie was indignant; her indignation gave way to tears; and still Harland waited. At length she blew her nose, wiped her eyes and cleared her throat. 'I am truthful,' she said. 'I am truthful.'

'Then tell me what Tony said to you the morning she died.'

'I wasn't there,' Jennie said stubbornly. 'I wasn't there. If Beatrice said she saw me, she's the one who is lying.'

Harland sighed. 'Beatrice is trying frantically to protect you. She has shut Mrs George's mouth so that she won't speak of the quarrel you had with Tony. She is covering your tracks like mad.'

'Oh, well,' Jennie said drearily, and she began to cry again, not tempestuous tears, not even pathetic tears, just a constant flooding and overflowing of her eyes like one of those gray, sodden rains that utterly depress the spirit.

'It was Miles,' she said. 'He's a hypocrite. I see that now. But he seemed to be so fine.' There was a bitter twist to her mouth. 'I thought he was above baseness, not taken in by bad women. Well, I found out different. I don't know what he and Tony were doing around the corner of the terrace, out of sight, all alone, but you saw how he looked when he came back, when he was caught!

'But I wasn't sure.' She wiped her cheek with the back of her hand in a childish gesture. 'I thought it was only fair to give him another chance. And,' her voice quavered, 'forgive him if it was just a moment of weakness. But I

212

didn't want to cheapen myself by telephoning him first. So, when he didn't call me, I went for a walk down Fifth Avenue.'

She met Harland's eyes and flushed scarlet. 'All right,' she said defiantly, 'I waited outside his house until he came out. And I followed him. He went straight to Carey's apartment. The door was open and I didn't see him and I—so I went downstairs to have it out with Tony. She was taking her bath and the radio was turned on loud. She looked at me and laughed.' Jennie wiped her eyes. 'Tony laughed,' she said again incredulously.

Harland offered her a cigarette which she refused and he lighted one for himself, taking his time.

'I asked her whether she expected to marry Miles and she said she could get what she wanted without that, thank God.' Jennie added by way of apology, 'That's what Tony said—thank God, I mean. And I said hadn't she done enough evil? And she screamed at me, "Get the hell out of here!" And I went. And she was alive when I left her. I swear it. She was alive. And I don't know what happened to Miles.'

'And last night?' Harland prompted her when he saw that she had come to a full stop. 'Last night when your mother thought you were with Carey?'

'I wasn't trying to make things up with Miles,' Jennie said, trying to cling to the last

213

shreds of her pride, 'only it seemed fair for us to talk about it. And I didn't want Mom to know I was going to look for him. She wouldn't understand that. People come to Mom without being asked.'

Harland turned his face away while he hunted for a place to deposit the ashes from his cigarette. At length he dropped them on the floor. Poor Jennie.

'So I told Mom I was going to see Carey and I went down past Miles's house again. I waited there for a long time—hours, I guess—but there weren't any lights.' She glanced at her watch. 'I've got to be uptown in an hour. I promised to mail circulars in Harlem for a charity group this afternoon.' She got up and met his eyes. 'Well, what do you think?' she said challengingly.

'On the whole,' Harland replied, 'it's a very fat baby.'

CHAPTER EIGHTEEN

All day Saturday Harland prowled restlessly around the house, upstairs, downstairs, pulling books off the shelves, glancing at them without knowing what he read, and abandoning them on tables, on chair arms, on the rug. It was enough, Mrs Larsen thought, to drive a body crazy. And the telephone going like mad.

'Out of town,' she told everybody, because she had her orders. Mr Harland would be back on Monday. No, she couldn't say where he might be reached.

It was the end of a case. She knew that much. And when Harland had nibbled at her asparagus hollandaise and pushed it away from him, almost untouched, she marched out to the kitchen, mixed a dose of bicarbonate of soda, and made him take it. Then she waited for the moment when he would tell her all about it, not because she could ever see how he worked it all out, but because in some way it helped him to put it into words.

Just like a child he is, she thought tolerantly.

She could hear him tramping up and down his room and at last he came down the circular staircase with his quick, light step. If you didn't see the white hair, he was almost like a boy with his slight figure and his youthful voice. He looked around almost as though expecting her to be there waiting for him.

'Oh, there you are, Mrs Larsen. Won't you come in and sit down while you listen to this? I'd like to know what you think of it.'

Mrs Larsen smiled to herself. For years he had been talking to her and not once had it occurred to him to ask her opinion.

'Yes, sir,' she said.

'You've read the newspaper stories, I suppose, about those two murders—Mrs Walker's and Oleson's?'

'Yes, sir.'

The telephone rang and when she returned he asked, 'Who was it this time?'

'Lieutenant Mattheson of Homicide. He said Mrs Walker's body is to be released for burial on Monday. The lieutenant said all information about the services would be withheld from the newspapers until afterwards so as to keep away curiosity seekers.'

'No,' Harland said quickly, 'that won't do. Tell him—wait, I'll talk to him myself.'

He came back at length and sat down. 'Ready?' he asked.

Mrs Larsen pulled some yarn from her pocket and began to knit. 'Yes, sir,' she said.

'Well,' Harland began, 'this story really started...'

Long before he had finished talking, twilight had fallen in the room, but Mrs Larsen did not need a light for her knitting, and the needles clicked softly, row after row of soft blue wool dropping onto her lap. When at length Harland stopped speaking she got up, rolled the knitting into a ball and went out to the kitchen. She came back with a highball and a chicken sandwich and switched on the lights.

'You didn't eat your lunch, sir.'

Harland's eyes were cloudy as though he were hardly aware of her. 'Thank you.' He reached for the glass, sipped it and pushed it away.

216

Mrs Larsen moved the plate with the sandwich so that it was in front of him and he smiled.

'I don't deserve you,' he said. 'Get something for yourself, and a drink. You'll need it after all that listening. Bring them back here.'

Mrs Larsen was shocked but she went out quietly, made herself a sandwich, poured a mild drink and came back to her chair.

'So there it is,' Harland said, 'and I can't prove it. There are no clues. Only motive. And character. But you can't face a jury with motive and character. The trouble is that a person who is clever can dress up red herrings and create evidence, build a case against an innocent person. You see that, don't you?'

'Yes, sir.' The housekeeper gave his plate a push and he ate his sandwich.

'A murderer whose life is at stake won't hesitate to produce evidence that would tell against an innocent person. And there were so many people who had sound reasons for wanting Tony out of the way. Even if the evidence is insufficient to convict them, the stigma would remain. No one emerges unscathed from a murder trial.' He rubbed the back of his neck that ached with tension. 'I've tried to stop all the holes but I'm not sure I have. What's the matter with the police? Why can't they produce Alvin? It's preposterous!'

He pulled out a pack of cards and Mrs

Larsen cleared the table, leaving only the highball glass, cigarette box and ashtray. He shuffled the cards and dealt them. A red nine on a black ten. Black eight on the red nine. Opens up a space.

On the other side of the table Mrs Larsen knitted. The needles clicked, clicked. In all these years Harland had never brought himself to tell his housekeeper that he loathed seeing a woman knit. It was a process he associated with the women who sat under the guillotine during the French Revolution, watching the heads of aristocrats drop into the basket. What was that? Watching—

'And I still,' he continued his thought aloud, 'have no actual knowledge of how Graham Aldrich died. Only a theory. Get Mr Morehouse on the telephone, will you, Mrs Larsen? We've got a job to do.'

A moment later she returned. 'Mr Morehouse asked if it was something he could do tomorrow instead, sir. He said Miss Walker had asked him to dinner tonight. He seemed quite excited about it.'

'No!' Harland said sharply. 'No! Tell him to cancel it. Tell him to pack a bag and come down here at once.'

She returned from the telephone to say, 'He'll be down in an hour, sir.'

'Make up a bed for him, Mrs Larsen. I don't care what room you give him so long as it has a key on the outside of the door. Morehouse is

218

going to stay under my eye if I have to lock him in.'

Mrs Larsen's lips parted.

'It won't do,' Harland insisted. 'A sudden reversal in Jennie's interests won't do at this point.'

'Yes, sir,' she said.

*   *   *

It was only half-past seven when Harland, accompanied by a sulky David, entered the Club Royale. At that hour there was nothing in the scene to raise their spirits. The tables were unoccupied, the musicians had not yet arrived, and their shrouded instruments slept under the dim lights. Four men talking together in low tones looked up as they came in.

Lieutenant Mattheson came forward to meet them and introduced his three companions: Murphy, the manager; Heindrich, the head waiter; and Carlos, the waiter who had had Graham Aldrich's table the night he was hurt. Then the lieutenant waved his hand.

'Take it away,' he said to Harland. 'This is your show.'

Murphy was a big man with massive shoulders and a broken nose, who looked like an ex-pugilist run to fat but still light on his feet. Heindrich was tall, bold, suave and deprecating in manner. Carlos was a Spaniard,

219

short, dark, with liquid eyes and a cheerful smile.

Harland looked around the room. 'Is this arranged the same way it was the night Graham Aldrich was hurt?'

'For the most part,' Murphy said. 'The only difference is the special tables.' He went on to explain that on the night in question five special tables had been set out at the rim of the dance floor.

'It was at the peak of the season and we were introducing a sensational new dance team, Lolita and José—they are in Hollywood now. Everything was booked up so we set out these tables for any special guests who might come along.'

'Suppose you do that now,' Harland suggested, 'so we'll have the correct picture without any guesswork.'

Murphy directed the two other men and in a few moments the tables had been placed in the proper position.

'Now,' Harland said, 'tell me in as much detail as you can exactly what happened.'

All three began at once and then the two waiters were silent, giving way to the manager.

'I didn't see the fight myself,' the manager said. 'I was back in the dressing rooms giving Lolita and José a pep talk before they went on because it was their first appearance in a big New York night spot and they were nervous. I was sent for when Aldrich had been knocked

220

out. When I came out, Aldrich was lying there beside his table—'

'Aldrich had this table?'

The head waiter nodded confirmation.

'Let's clarify things,' Harland suggested, 'and designate these tables, A, B, C, D, and E. Now then, Aldrich was at table D. Carry on.'

'There was a lot of confusion,' the manager continued. 'People were milling around. I didn't see anything that led up to the fight so I can't tell you about that. I wasn't much disturbed about it because Aldrich was always a trouble raiser and we'd sent him home drunk before. So Heindrich and Carlos carried him out the side entrance and put him in a cab for home.'

'Did you feel his pulse?' Harland asked.

Murphy looked disgusted. 'No, nor hold his hand either.'

Harland turned to the head waiter. 'What can you add to that?'

Heindrich enjoyed the center of the stage. 'Mr Aldrich came quite late and he was tearing drunk. I gave him this table D.'

'By the way, who had the other tables?'

Heindrich considered for a moment. 'Tim Oleson, the night-club man, got table A. That was good business because he'd have given us a column on the new show the next day if Aldrich hadn't been hurt.' He thought for a moment. There was a couple at table E, but they had nothing to do with this.'

'Do you remember who they were?'

'Old Templeton, the architect, and a girl.'

'How do you happen to remember?'

'Templeton didn't want any publicity and he gave me fifty dollars to keep his name out of it.' Heindrich glanced at Lieutenant Mattheson and added quickly, 'I didn't see any harm in it. Templeton was an old man and he couldn't have had anything to do with the fight. Anyhow, he died of a stroke a few weeks later.'

'How about the other tables?'

'Table C,' Heindrich said, 'had a honeymoon couple. Out-of-towners who talked with a southern accent. Table B—' he shook his head. 'I don't remember. Oh, yes, I do. Fellow came in alone and wanted a table. I didn't know him so I said we were booked up. He got nasty and pushed his way in and saw this empty table. So he just sat down and said the only way I'd get him out would be to throw him out.' Heindrich shrugged. 'We didn't want trouble here and he looked as though he could pay so I let it ride. Only way to stop the scene he was making.'

'Well, tell me what you saw.'

'Aldrich was sitting so he faced the bride at table C and he began to get fresh with her, tried to make her dance with him and then began calling things to her. The girl's husband got sore and told him to quit it or he'd sock him one. So I whispered to him who Mr Aldrich was and he didn't want any trouble with a big

222

shot so he just tried to ignore the whole thing.

'Well, Aldrich liked to attract attention and when he found he wasn't stirring up enough, he grabbed a bottle and threw it at this guy and the fun started. By the time I got there, Aldrich was out cold so we carried him off the floor.'

Harland's expression was ludicrous in its consternation. 'You mean that it was this bridegroom at table C who struck Aldrich?'

'I didn't see who struck him,' Heindrich said. 'Well, Carlos?'

'I saw the whole thing,' Carlos said eagerly, 'Mr Aldrich throws this bottle, see, but his aim isn't so good on account of he's dead drunk, so he hits the guy who is sitting alone at table B. And this guy moves like lightning. He pushes back his chair, makes a jump for Aldrich, hauls him up and throws one of the hardest punches I ever saw. Aldrich just folded up.'

'This man at table B,' Harland said eagerly. 'Do you know who he was?'

Carlos shook his head. 'He came in alone and he was gone by the time the excitement was over. I've never seen him here since.'

Harland looked thoughtfully at the five special tables. 'But the man who struck Aldrich and did the vanishing act was sitting at the next table to Oleson. Therefore, Oleson must have got a good look at him.'

'Oleson,' the manager put in bitterly, 'never missed anything that had the makings of a scandal. He could smell it out.'

'I suppose,' Harland said, 'there was no question in anyone's mind about Aldrich's real condition—how badly he had been hurt?'

'We took it for granted he'd just been knocked out and he'd be all right by the time he sobered up,' Murphy said.

Harland pulled out the front page of the tabloid, which had begun to look the worse for wear. 'Have you ever seen this girl?'

They bent over the picture, 'That's her,' Heindrich exclaimed. 'That's the girl who was with old Templeton at table E.'

Carlos nodded. 'Yeah, that's the one. She has the kind of face you remember.' His eyes traveled down the page and stopped at Carey's photograph. 'That's the guy at table B—the one who socked Graham Aldrich.'

CHAPTER NINETEEN

Joe Pelozzi, the taxi driver, was small, with a sharp nose, deep wrinkles in his forehead, and an unshaven face. Yes, sure he remembered taking Graham Aldrich home. He had gone over it with the police so often he could tell it in his sleep. He was cruising when the doorman at the Club Royale blew his whistle and then Heindrich and Carlos had come out the side entrance, carrying the guy, put him on the back seat and given Pelozzi the Aldrich address on

Fifth Avenue.

When he had reached his destination, Joe tried to rouse his fare, decided he was too drunk to navigate, and rang the bell for help. The butler had come down, acted as though it was an old story, and together they had got Aldrich into the house, up the elevator to his room on the third floor where another man— 'Dis guy's so dumb he needs a fellow to undress him'—came in and said he would look after him. 'And he didn't like dis Aldrich. Sour as if his mother's milk had curdled in him.' The butler had seen him out, given him a nice tip and that was all.

'Are you able to swear,' Harland asked, 'that the man was alive when you put him down in his room?'

Joe rubbed his unshaven jaw with a rasping sound. 'I just thought he'd passed out.'

'Did you put him on his bed?'

'No, dis noisemaid and I slung him on one of dem long chairs.'

When the taxi driver had been dismissed with a generous tip, the three men were silent. The lieutenant was thoughtful, David puzzled, and Harland's spirit wavered between a profound depression and a sense of elation that his theory was proving to have a solid foundation in fact.

'I get it,' Mattheson said at length. 'Carey Walker was the guy who knocked out Graham Aldrich. You are trying to prove that Walker

225

killed him; that Antonia Smith, who had picked up old man Templeton, saw it happen and blackmailed Walker into marrying her. Then Oleson saw them together, remembered them, figured out Tony's racket, and put the squeeze on her.'

The lieutenant thought for a moment. 'Then Walker gets tired of his bargain and kills his wife. Oleson points the finger at him and he kills Oleson.' He shook his head. 'Very ingenious,' he said. 'There's only one thing wrong with it. It's not so.'

'What's the weak spot?' Harland asked.

'Graham Aldrich was alive when he got home. You haven't talked to his valet yet and I have. We went through all this last year. If you can shake his evidence you're good. Second place, maybe Walker could have killed Oleson—he hasn't an alibi. But he sure as hell has one for the time when his wife was killed and—if your theory is correct—only one person committed both murders.'

'Only one,' Harland agreed. 'May I give you a drink before you go?'

Mattheson shook his head regretfully. 'On my way to spend Saturday evening—what's left of it—with my wife's aunt. She's a pillar of the W.C.T.U.'

'And now what?' David asked when the lieutenant had gone. He did not endeavor to hide his grievance over missing dinner with Jennie.

226

'And now,' Harland said, 'we are going to talk to the man who was Graham Aldrich's valet.'

David gave him a curious glance. 'You are hard to convince.'

'It has to be this way,' Harland said. 'It simply has to. Graham's valet is a man named Burns, a bit of a rabble rouser who makes speeches. We'll find him at Bridges Hall.' As he saw David's open mouth he looked amused. 'No magic,' he said. 'I learned all that by the simple expedient of asking Mattheson.'

They sauntered through the Village and up the worn stairs of a dingy walk-up smelling of cabbage, garlic, and mice, to the third floor where empty benches awaited an audience. At one end of the room there was a speaker's stand cluttered with pamphlets. On the wall hung a large American flag surrounded by agitated placards warning that the American way of life was being attacked on all sides and had practically reached its last gasp.

There was only one person in the room, a big man with dark bushy hair and fierce eyes, minus coat and necktie, sorting pamphlets. He turned and stared at them with hostility.

'The meeting doesn't start until ten o'clock.'

'Your name is Burns, isn't it?'

'What of it?' His name, Burns implied, was his own property and not to be employed lightly by strangers. 'And this is no rich man's club; it's for workers.'

Harland nodded. 'So I understand.'

'What do you want with me?'

'A few minutes of your valuable time.'

Burns sat down on a bench. 'All right,' he said grudgingly, 'what is it?'

'You were Graham Aldrich's valet, weren't you?'

'That's right. I slave so the playboy won't have to decide what suit to put on.'

'You were there the night he died, weren't you?'

'Ask the police. I told them the whole story. Am I supposed to cry because he drinks himself to death?'

'I suppose,' Harland said sharply, 'you are positive that Aldrich was alive when he reached the house.'

'I'm positive, all right.' There was an ugly expression on Burns's face. 'He hit me.'

The change in Harland's expression was ludicrous. 'He hit you?' he said aghast. 'Impossible! He couldn't have.'

'He did, though. And not the first time either.'

David glanced at Harland and decided not to speak. The old boy had the wind up.

Harland's fingers beat a nervous tattoo on the bench. 'But then nothing makes any sense. Man,' he said earnestly, 'he couldn't have hit you.' His eyes begged Burns to retract his words.

'Well, he did,' Burns said sullenly. 'What

difference does it make now?'

'The butler and the taxi driver carried him up to his room in the elevator,' Harland said. 'Where did they put him?'

'On the chaise longue.' As Harland waited, Burns went on, rationing his words as sparingly as though they were articles of food in post-war Europe. 'I started to undress him and he struck me and I thought, the hell with it, let him undress himself, so I went up to my room and left him.'

'And when did you discover that he was dead?'

'In the morning. I went in and found him lying on the floor. I told Aldrich and he sent for a doctor. The doc said his neck was broken and checked up on the night before and heard about the fight at the night club. They worked it out—the police and the doctor and Aldrich—that Graham came home with a broken neck and then dies at home.' He laughed. 'Trust Miles Aldrich. He'd get himself out of a gas chamber safely. When we get a people's government—'

There was a long pause while Harland considered the ex-valet and the latter fidgeted. 'I take it,' Harland said at length, 'you are implying that Graham received the fatal injury *after* he got home.'

'Don't try picking at my words,' Burns said excitedly. 'You asked what happened. I told you.'

'Did you?' Harland said gently.

'So you're another of them,' Burns said bitterly. 'Another of the idle rich trying to get a poor man into trouble. Just so long as Miles Aldrich isn't suspected. Oh, no,' he said with heavy irony, 'not Miles Aldrich.'

Harland met David's eyes and raised his brows. 'It looks as though you were right,' he said solemnly.

Without quite knowing what was expected of him, David nodded his head. This by-play was not lost on Burns.

'How about getting out of here,' he said, standing up. 'I got friends coming to the meeting later on, and if they find you messing in my affairs—'

'I don't think it would be wise to involve your friends. Bad enough having the Homicide Squad interested in you without calling on the Federal boys.'

'What do you mean—Homicide?'

'I suggest,' Harland said, as though he had not heard the interruption, 'that Graham Aldrich was dead when he reached his house that night and that you knew it when you started to undress him.'

'That's a lie.'

'I suggest,' Harland went on, 'that you put his body on the floor where it was found, hoping that your testimony might get Miles Aldrich into trouble.'

'Why would I do that?'

230

'It does seem stupid,' Harland admitted. 'And it didn't work, did it?'

David, watching, saw that Harland was delicately goading at Burns who had little emotional control at best.

'You don't think the police would touch Miles Aldrich, do you?' Burns sneered. 'They weren't interested.'

'On the contrary,' Harland said. 'They were greatly interested. They still are. As a matter of fact, I got your present address from them. They are interested in your meetings here. You see, if it is true that Graham was alive when he reached home, and received his fatal injury afterwards, there is only one logical suspect, and that is the man with a grievance, the man who claims that Graham Aldrich struck him.'

Burns's head snapped back as though he had received a physical blow. 'Look,' he said hoarsely, 'that's not true. They can't pin that on me. They—'

'Who else?' Harland asked.

'Look,' Burns began again desperately. He rubbed his forehead with his hand. 'Look—you don't know what it's like, see? Graham hit me often enough. Once he even threw a shoe and cut my cheekbone. And his brother gave me orders and called me, "My good man." And I got a bellyful. So—' he swallowed—'when I came to undress Graham that night I saw he was dead. At first, I was going to call his brother and then I thought I'd give him

231

something to worry about for once in his life. So I put Graham down on the floor, so the butler would see he'd moved in the night and then I just—stuck to my story that he had been alive when he got home. I thought I'd let Miles do some explaining. You can't do anything to me for that. You—'

'He was dead,' Harland said happily. He pulled out his wallet and slipped a bill into Burns's hand. 'For the cause,' he said cryptically and went down the stairs at such a pace that David had to run to catch up with him.

*   *   *

By ten o'clock Sunday morning a line had already formed outside the Jensen Undertaking Parlor on upper Broadway where, according to announcements in all the newspapers, Mrs Carey Walker's body could be seen by the public. By five in the afternoon, the line stretched to the end of the block and around the corner, with a couple of policemen to maintain order and see that they kept moving. There were other policemen on hand but not in uniform and they made themselves as inconspicuous as possible. One of them stood in the back of the room beside a stout, elderly woman.

'All you have to do, Mrs Jacobs,' he said, 'is to wave your handkerchief when you spot him.

Got it?'

She nodded her gray head in reply. Before he moved away toward the door, the policeman warned her, 'But keep your mind on what you're doing. Don't let him get past you.'

'I won't,' she said.

One by one, the crowd shuffled through the doors and past the casket where Tony lay. The undertaker had been more adept than Mrs George at covering the marks of bruises, but then he had a different clientele.

'Where do they come from?' David whispered to Harland from behind a row of potted palms. 'What do they get out of this?'

Harland shook his head without taking his eyes off the slow procession of morbid curiosity-seekers. Most of them were well-dressed, cheerful looking women; a few were derelicts; there was an occasional man. It was the men Harland watched. In all these hours he had seen only two familiar faces, and both had surprised him. He had expected neither Mrs Harrison Ives nor Miles Aldrich to be part of that line. Both of them paused to gaze at Tony's still face and moved on without being aware of the hidden eyes that followed them.

'He's not coming,' David said wearily. 'He'd have been here before this. Seven hours we've been waiting.' His fingers plucked at Harland's sleeve. 'Look!' he whispered.

Mrs George was conspicuous among the women because of her beautiful carriage, her severely smart clothes, her lacquered hair and carefully made-up face. She was really, Harland reflected, a splendid advertisement for her business. She reached the casket and paused, her face completely unrevealing. Then she went on.

Another ten minutes passed and David gave a stifled exclamation. Harland followed his eyes and saw Jennie Walker clinging to Beatrice Comstock's arm. They were nearly opposite the concealed men. Having reached her destination, Jennie was afraid to look. She stood with eyes closed, swaying.

'She's going to faint,' Harland warned David, and the latter darted around the screen of palms and caught the girl's arm.

Jennie gave a half cry and then began to sob. David, murmuring soothing words, pushed his way through the crowd and led her outside, where a photographer snapped a picture of the weeping girl.

The doors were to be closed to the public at eight o'clock. By seven, even Harland wondered whether his idea had missed fire. He had been so sure that it would work. If Alvin was 'crazy mad' about Tony, as Mrs Jacobs had testified, he would come. He was bound to come. And yet Harland would have taken his oath that Alvin had not slipped past him unnoticed in the line.

And then he saw Margaret Walker, her hand gripping Carey's arm. For a long moment the two stood there and then Carey said gently, 'Come on, Mom. Come on.'

Harland's eyes followed them—the tall, good-looking man with the chalk-white face and the slight woman with frightened eyes.

A few moments later his attention was attracted by movement in the back of the room. Mrs Jacobs was waving her handkerchief. Harland followed her eyes and saw an inconspicuous man standing before the casket, his gaunt face covered by a stubble of beard, his lips moving soundlessly.

The policeman had slipped outside and when the man emerged and drifted away into the twilight the policeman moved away from the side of the building and followed him.

*　　*　　*

Alvin walked up Broadway in the gathering dusk and turned toward Riverside Drive. The sky was opaline. On the Hudson, a fat ferry boat, like a lighted birthday cake, waddled from the Jersey shore; pleasure craft lay at anchor; the swish, swish, of the unending line of traffic down below on the parkway; bright, neon signs on the Jersey shore blinking on and off.

For Alvin the river was empty. The world was empty. He saw nothing but a girl's waxen face with closed eyes. There were no lights twinkling on the broad breast of the Hudson, no afterglow in the sky. There was only darkness.

After a long while Alvin moved on, stumbling, uncertain. And the policeman followed, steadily, implacably, infinitely patient.

It was nearly nine o'clock when Alvin turned away from Riverside Drive and plodded toward Broadway. Not a glamorous Broadway this far north. A section of delicatessens and second-run movie theaters, of cheap clothing houses, ubiquitous drugstores, grocery stores with vegetables wilting out of doors.

The sight of the food forced its way into his numb mind and his mouth watered. In the window of a neighborhood restaurant a white-capped chef turned a chicken on a spit and at a table a man tied his napkin sturdily around his neck, fished up spaghetti on a fork, rolled it onto the spoon in his left hand and popped it into his mouth, drawing in the last trailing bit with a practiced inhalation that left a stream of tomato sauce on his chin. Alvin swallowed.

He moved on jerkily. For the first time he became aware of the sound of footsteps. They had accompanied him for a long time, he could not remember how long. They seemed always to have been there. He went on and the footsteps followed after. He halted and the footsteps halted.

Alvin began to run, not fast because he was

too weak, but wildly, without direction. The footsteps were quicker now, they broke into a trot. Alvin started blindly across the street, heard the screaming of brakes, and saw a dark shape loom over him. He flung up an arm to cover his face.

'I couldn't have stopped,' the bus driver said over and over. 'I couldn't have stopped. He shot out right under the wheels.'

'It's not your fault,' the policeman said. 'No one was to blame.'

In Alvin's pocket he found the emerald necklace.

CHAPTER TWENTY

'Mrs George will see you now,' the receptionist said in a hushed voice, and she led the way into the Presence.

Mrs George came forward to meet Harland, her hand outstretched, the neon light flashing. 'How nice of you to come,' she said with her careful enunciation. 'I remember our meeting at the Walkers' cocktail party.' The bold eyes fluttered in an unsuccessful effort to assume shyness. 'I'm so glad that you remembered too.' Her tone transformed the business office into a boudoir—but a boudoir with a cash register.

All that cosmetics, diet, exercise, corseting

and expensive clothes could do for a middle-aged woman had been done for Mrs George. She was handsome from the carefully dyed black hair to the hand-made shoes in which her feet appeared a size smaller.

'I hoped that by coming at this hour I might persuade you to have cocktails with me,' Harland said.

She gave his clothes a swift, shrewd appraisal and said, 'How delightful!'

'Would the Plaza suit you or have you another choice?'

The Plaza, it appeared, was her favorite place for cocktails.

Escorting Mrs George was rather like sallying forth with a hawk, Harland thought, watching the predatory eyes light on a woman, rip her apart and drop on another victim with the same deadly aim.

To his surprise, she proved to be a moderate drinker. Her figure was more important than her thirst. And she was better company than he had anticipated. In the course of an eventful career she had learned that she was expected to pay for what she received, and she set herself the task of amusing him. She was cheerful, her observations astute, her comments good humored and genuinely funny.

While she left her second cocktail untouched, Harland sipped his own, wondering how to broach the question he had come to ask. The time had passed to beat around the bush.

'I sent Alvin to his death as surely as though I had pushed him in front of that truck,' Harland had told Mattheson when the latter telephoned to say the body had been found and identified by Mrs Jacobs. Harland lashed himself with bitter words. 'I was the one who wanted to smoke him out, to lure him up to the undertaker's to see Tony's body.'

There was nothing left now but to block off the last false trail. And get proof. Two murders and not a shred of evidence to take before a jury. Not a witness.

Yes, there was one witness, a witness who would never talk. Harland's jaw set. A witness who must be forced to talk.

'I suppose you are aware,' he told Mrs George, 'that I have been investigating the murder of Mrs Carey Walker.'

Mrs George's face fell. 'Really? You don't look like a detective. Mrs Walker told me you were someone famous.'

'I'm not a detective,' he assured her, 'but now and then I take a hand in a case that interests me.'

'It has taken you a long time to get around to me,' she said dryly.

Harland smiled, 'You've been outside my calculations; first, because you had an alibi; now, because we've come to the end of our trail.'

'You know who did it.' Mrs George did not

ask a question, she stated a fact.

'Yes, I know. I've known for some time, but I couldn't prove it. So I waited for evidence.'

Mrs George watched his mobile face curiously. 'I haven't the faintest idea what you are talking about.'

'I'm talking about the fact that there is a murderer at large: a murderer who electrocuted Tony Walker and smashed the skull of Tim Oleson—because they got in the murderer's way.' Harland added more slowly, his eyes riveted on hers, 'Because they knew things.'

He finished his drink. 'That's why the murderer must be stopped. It's why I have come to you. Because you know something that it is dangerous for you to know.'

Mrs George nodded. 'Yes,' she said. 'I figured that.'

'I understand from Miss Comstock that, in exchange for a certain memorandum, you promised not to mention Jennie Walker's quarrel with Mrs Carey Walker. Is that true?'

'Here's where I put my cards on the table,' Mrs George said coolly. 'I'm not mixing in murder.'

'Very sensible of you.'

'It's like this. I kept still in the first place because I figured it was healthier not to talk; now, if you know who the murderer is, I might as well speak my piece. Miss Comstock talked about Jennie but that's not what she had on her mind. She was worried about Carey Walker. He was my alibi like I was his. Well, the truth is that Mr Walker had an appointment with me Thursday at eleven but he never showed up. He's got no alibi at all. And Miss Comstock knew it.'

Harland signaled for his check. 'Thank you, Mrs George. Forgive me if I leave you without ceremony but there's no time to lose.'

Her eyes followed him as he crossed the room, walking with a purposeful air. She shivered. Then she reached for her second cocktail.

*　　　*　　　*

Carey poured himself a drink at the bar and carried it out onto the terrace. Even at this height there was no breeze. Not a leaf stirred on the bushes. He set his glass on the railing and looked out at the glittering towers, then down at the East River.

Down. When you stared like this, space seemed to reach out for you, to call you, to pull you down. Out of the whole filthy mess. They said you were conscious while you fell. Until you landed and there was nothing left of you. Nothing left of Carey Walker. And a good job, too.

He stood with a hand on either side of him resting on the rail, leaning far over. He did not hear the key turn in the lock or the closing of the door. He did not hear the light, rapid footsteps cross the living-room and come to a sudden halt.

Then with a rush Beatrice was at his side. For a moment he hung half over the barrier, legs flailing as he clutched at the railing. Then he flung himself backward and landed on the floor of the terrace, his weight bearing Beatrice down with him.

'Carey,' she sobbed. 'Carey. Oh, God, what were you doing? If I hadn't been in time, you'd have gone over.'

He picked himself up and brushed off his suit. 'Nonsense,' he said lazily. 'I was just looking. You startled me. Don't be so impetuous, Trix.'

She sank down on the foot-rest of a long chair, her face ashen. Under the large dark eyes the marks of fatigue and strain stood like bruises.

'What were you doing?' she asked again.

'Thinking that it's a hell of a long way to the bottom,' he said lightly.

'But you wouldn't—Carey, you wouldn't have—'

He looked at her in silence. They had always known each other's thoughts. Extra-sensory perception, she called it. Odd how well they had always understood each other.

He was on his knees beside her without knowing how he got there, his arms straining around her, his face pressed against her breast.

It was a terrible thing to hear a man cry.

'Don't,' she whispered. 'Don't, my dearest. It's all over. It's all right now. It's all right.' She bent over, brushing her cheek against his hair.

His arms released her abruptly and he got to his feet. His face was marble-white, his eyes red-rimmed and bloodshot.

'Are you mad?' he said, his voice colorless, spent. 'Are you blind?'

'What do you mean?' Automatically her fingertips touched her forehead, smoothing out the little pucker between the beautifully arched brows.

'Do you believe for a moment it's all right?'

Beatrice came to stand beside him. She slipped her hand under his arm. 'Of course it's all right,' she said firmly. 'There isn't a thing for you to worry about, Carey. Even if anyone suspected, there isn't a scrap of proof. It's all over.'

'Why did you call in John Harland?'

Beatrice let her hand slip from his arm. 'Because you were there,' she said simply. 'Because I realized you hadn't gone out. You didn't have an alibi. And I was afraid the police would think you had done it.'

'There's nothing like a woman's mind,' Carey said. 'I suppose you know now that you made a mistake.'

'How?'

'Because,' Carey said expressionlessly, 'John Harland is going to send you to the electric chair.'

'Carey!' The agony in her voice left him unmoved. For the first time she did not know what he was thinking. 'Carey,' she said, her voice hardly above a whisper, 'you couldn't do that to me. Not and be you. Say you don't mean it. I love you. For seven years I've loved you. Even when you asked for a divorce, even when I went on working here day after day, with Tony in my place, taunting me, I loved you. And every hour of it was sheer hell.'

'Why did you insist on going on with the work?'

'Because I had to be near you; I had to see you. It wasn't much but it was all I had. I couldn't give that up. And then when I saw what was happening to you, the way you were drinking, letting the business slip, getting demoralized, I thought I could help you. Why didn't you tell me the truth about her, Carey?'

'What difference would it have made?' His voice was flat. 'I suppose you know now how it happened. It was the night you and I quarreled about the Milton girl because I'd been out with her on business and you were jealous. You kept at me and at me until I couldn't stand it any more. So I did some pub crawling. I was sore all the way through and felt like scrapping; you'd been running me so much I wanted to take it out on someone else.

'Well, I ended up at the Club Royale and they said it was booked up. Ordinarily, I'd have gone somewhere else but that night I had to have my own way. So I raised a row and got one of the special tables on the dance floor. By that time I was stinking drunk and I don't remember clearly what happened. All I know is that Graham Aldrich came in, threw a bottle at someone, hit me and I knocked him down.

'The next day I picked up the paper and read that he was dead. He'd had his neck broken and I knew I'd killed him. That was bad enough. All my life people have said, "Watch your temper, Carey. Some day it will get you into trouble." And while I was wondering what in hell to do about it, Tony came to see me. She'd been at the night club with some old guy she'd picked up, saw the quarrel and followed me home to find out who I was. Her escort had told her about Aldrich and she figured it for blackmail. I was in a panic already because I couldn't remember. I didn't know whether I'd provoked the quarrel or not and you couldn't tell from the papers what had happened exactly.'

Carey turned his back on Beatrice and stood looking out over the city. 'So I was a pushover,' he said at length. 'I'd blacked out completely; all I could remember was being drunk and tangling with someone. I couldn't remember the details. But what I did remember was that I had wanted to fight and that I'd been killing mad when I left home. So—' He turned back, his manner impassive, detached.

'So Tony put the screws on. Either I'd marry her or I'd go to prison for manslaughter. She had it figured out. She'd seen the fuss I made when I forced the waiter to give me a table. How could I prove I hadn't planned the whole thing—premeditation?

'If I'd used any sense at all I'd have known it wouldn't hold up. But—how the hell can I explain. I *felt* guilty so I thought I was. And I asked you for a divorce and married her. If it's any satisfaction to you, I hated her.'

He went into the living-room and in a few minutes returned with two highballs.

'When I came,' Beatrice said at last, 'what were you thinking?'

'That death wasn't the worst thing that could happen to me,' Carey said grimly. 'Thinking of the harm I'd done.' There was a queer expression on his face, one she had never seen before, that she did not know how to interpret.

'Harland knows,' he said. 'I saw it in his face the night Oleson—died. He knew when I made that telephone call to you, establishing your alibi. I broke the connection so he wouldn't hear the ringing, but he could hear the dial tone. He knew there was no one at the other end of the line. Trix, for God's sake, wasn't there any other way? Did you have to kill them?'

246

CHAPTER TWENTY-ONE

Through the dull throbbing of his pain Carey was acutely aware of her. He knew her more completely than he had ever known anyone in his life. Her body held no reserves, no mystery for him; her mind had been a supplement of his own. They had laughed and fought and loved each other. And now he looked at her and wondered who she was, what she was.

'I don't know,' Beatrice said wearily. She sank back into one of the terrace chairs with her familiar grace, black hair flawlessly arranged, outwardly unruffled. Only her eyes were different, the huge eyes that had been her one beauty, and were now as blank as the sightless eyes of a statue.

'I want to tell you about it but I don't know how to explain. These last two days I've kept saying to myself, "You are a murderer," and it doesn't mean anything. It doesn't make any sense at all. People like us don't commit murder. Only—there it is.'

'But why?' Carey groaned. 'Why?'

'It wasn't like the books,' she said, struggling painfully to find an answer for him, an answer for herself. 'It wasn't a big thing. It was an accumulation of little ones. I loved you and wanted you and it was torment seeing you with her, thinking you loved her, seeing what she was doing to you—the drinking, the unhappiness, the business neglected. Seeing her youth, knowing that I was growing old. Ever since our marriage, age has been my enemy because you were five years younger.

'A few months ago I'd rather have died than tell you this. Anyhow, I had got used to it. Sometimes I would feel cheerful enough and life would seem possible. Then there were times when I couldn't bear it another moment. The way you feel doesn't have much to do with outward circumstances. It's something that happens inside. And the heat wave broke down my energy and vitality and hopefulness.' Her slim hands moved helplessly. 'Little things that added up.

'Well, you and I went to see Mrs Harrison Ives about the new contract and she made it clear she was afraid of blackmail—and I thought it was you she feared.'

'Trix!'

'I'm sorry. It just never occurred to me that it was Tony. I thought you were trying to get more money to satisfy Tony. That's when I began to think about killing her, not just wishing it. Really thinking of it. And yet, Carey, even when I thought of it, part of me didn't believe it at all. And then at the cocktail party she kept reminding me that she was hostess; she was your wife; I was older than you. And she pulled that trick with Miles.

'The next morning you came to my desk and

I knew you were fed up with her and you said something—that my eyes were still the loveliest in the world—and I knew then that I was going to kill her. You'd never have got rid of her and I wanted you back. And you had that appointment with Mrs George to provide you with an alibi if anything went wrong.'

'But what,' Carey demanded, 'did you think would happen to you—alone here and with no alibi at all?'

She was silent for a moment, sipping her drink. 'It's queer,' she said, 'it never occurred to me that people would think it was anything but an accident. I've read several cases of people dying that way—a radio falling into the tub, and no one ever said anything about murder. And even now, Carey, there isn't a single clue for the police. Whatever they may suspect they could never convict me. I was too careful. When I went in I spoke to Tony and washed my hands and reached back of her for a bath towel. I picked up the radio in the towel. I thought of all the angles—except that the radio was set in those grooves, and that you wouldn't have an alibi and that you were the one who had beaten her.'

She shivered. 'That's why I felt there was someone watching me in the office; you were there.'

'I was there,' Carey said. 'The heat and the radio blaring and Tony carrying on with Miles—it got me down. I didn't care whether we got the George contract or not. I went back to my room and tried to think things out. I was in a cleft stick whatever I did. If I broke with Tony she would tell Miles that I had killed Graham. Knowing Miles, I realized that would be the end of Jennie's happiness. And yet there must be some way you and I could rebuild something for ourselves. So I was going to tell you the whole thing, but you were standing at the window—all of a sudden you seemed like a stranger and I couldn't say anything. I went back to my room.'

'And all along you knew I had killed Tony.' Beatrice said.

'Yes, I knew.'

'Murder sounds like something special. And then it's just dropping a radio into a tub of water. Almost ridiculously easy. But almost at once, things began to go wrong. You were there when you should have been blocks away. The police discovered that the radio couldn't have fallen. And Jennie had come to see Tony, so I had to clear her somehow. I knew you'd never allow Jennie to suffer. So I made Mrs George promise to keep still about Jennie and back up your alibi. The way you backed me up when Oleson—died. How did you know I'd done that?'

'I didn't,' Carey said, 'but I couldn't take a chance. Because I knew you'd killed Tony. I didn't know anything about Oleson, but when Harland rushed in to say he'd been killed, I knew Oleson must have some connection with Tony because it was her death Harland was investigating. So I played safe.'

Beatrice explained how David had discovered Oleson's presence at the Club Royale the night Graham had been killed, that he was the T.O. who had made Tony go to the opening of the Frolic so he could talk to her, and how he had telephoned to Miles.

'You see, Oleson knew you had a terrific motive for killing Tony and I went to see him. Oleson thought you were guilty. He was nervous and he kept wandering around the room while he talked. Each time he sat down I noticed it was quite an effort for him because the couches were low and he was so stout. So I began to wander too and when he was sitting down I picked up the fire tongs—'

She saw his face then. 'It was for you, Carey! It was for you!'

There was a feeling of hollowness in the pit of Carey's stomach. He eased himself into a chair, put down the glass whose contents splashed over the side, and gripped his head in his hands.

'There's no proof,' she told him. 'I thought of all the angles. There's no proof.'

'Did you think,' Carey asked, 'that the police would just drop it?'

'No,' she said slowly, 'but there is the burglar and there is Miles.'

'Would you throw them to the police?' he

251

asked curiously.

'I don't see,' she said in surprise, 'why you should feel that way about Miles. You've never liked him.'

'No,' Carey said quietly. 'I never liked Miles. But you don't throw an innocent man to the wolves because you don't like him.'

'But—' She looked up, her eyes widening, and summoned her big, warm smile. 'Why, John! I didn't hear you come in. You're just in time for a drink.'

Harland came around the side of the terrace. Over his shoulder, Carey caught sight of the silent men behind him and he made no move toward the bar.

Harland looked down at Beatrice and said an unexpected thing. 'Hungry eyes! You had them even as a child. That's how I recognized you after so many years.' For a long moment he studied her, absently tapping a cigarette on the back of his case.

'I've come to report,' he said.

'How official you sound, John.' She was amused.

His gaunt face was profoundly sad. 'This is official, Beatrice. There is a price attached to murder, a heavy price, and it has to be paid.'

'How quick you've been,' she said.

'No, I've been too slow. The murderer moved too fast for me. In five days there have been two murders and a third was averted by a hair's breadth.'

'A third,' Carey exclaimed hoarsely. 'You're crazy.'

'I had begun to think,' Harland said, 'that I had failed entirely; there was not a clue, not a witness. When Tony died there were too many motives. I had an embarrassingly long list of suspects: Mrs Harrison Ives, Mrs Hazel George, Miles Aldrich, an unknown burglar, Beatrice and Jennie and Carey. All of you had reasons for wanting Tony out of the way. Because of that open, unguarded door, any one of you had access to the apartment undetected, and could have killed her. The only alibis were those of Carey and Mrs George; we knew that Beatrice and Miles were on the scene. In time, we learned that Jennie had been here too.

'Then Tim Oleson was killed. Only Mrs George had an alibi for that killing. You never fooled me, Carey, on that telephone call to Beatrice. In fact, it was that call.... However, we could eliminate most of our suspects. Mrs Harrison Ives, Mrs George, Jennie, the unknown burglar—none of them had any known motive for killing Oleson. That left three people: Carey, Beatrice, Miles. But Carey was alibied for the first murder, which, to our minds, eliminated him as a suspect from the second, because there was no reason to believe there were two murderers.

'And then,' Harland went on, 'we broke down Carey's alibi for the first murder. Mrs George has changed her mind and admitted that he did not keep his appointment with her that morning.'

Harland looked at his bony hands and Carey looked at Beatrice who looked at nothing at all. Harland sighed. 'Anything to say?' he asked. There was no sound at all on the terrace.

'But this is preposterous,' Beatrice said at last. 'You have no proof, John! You can't convict anyone without proof.' And when he made no reply, she insisted, 'Not without evidence. Not without witnesses.'

Harland's eyes were bleak. 'I'm sorry,' he said. 'I had hoped to spare you this. We come now to the third attempt at murder. Shall I go on, Beatrice?'

'Why not? Let's hear the rest of this fantastic accusation.'

'The third attempt came when you realized that Mrs George would not keep still about Carey's lack of alibi after she realized that she herself was in no danger. You had to silence the only witness who could testify against you, the only person who can prove you murdered Tony. That last attempt came less than half an hour ago when you tried to push Carey over the railing while you were pretending to save him from suicide. We have been here for some time.'

'No!' Carey cried. 'No!'

Beatrice said nothing at all.

'Carey,' Harland said sharply, 'what

happened the morning Tony died?'

'I was here, of course,' Carey said in a dead voice. 'I never left the apartment. Tony had the radio on full blast. I heard someone come down—I know now it was Jennie—and Tony screamed at her. Then I heard Beatrice go in. After awhile Freda came down and she yelled. I went in then.'

'*When did the radio stop?*'

'After Beatrice went in,' Carey said.

*   *   *

'Just the same,' Margaret Walker declared, 'you've got to eat. It's bad enough to have Carey trying to drink himself to death.'

'He's young,' Harland said, 'and resilient. Give him time. He has to work it out for himself. Right now he is completely sunk under a sense of guilt because, as he sees it, he is primarily responsible for what happened. He feels that Beatrice committed those crimes for him. And it is easier for Carey to face his own imaginary guilt than to accept the fact that Beatrice deliberately tried to kill him.'

'I never liked her,' Margaret said, 'and yet I thought she loved Carey.'

'She did, but there are many kinds of loving. Beatrice's kind was shaped and twisted by self-love. That came first. Love can be a destroyer as well as a creator.'

To please Margaret he accepted another

waffle. 'As it has been creative for Jennie,' he added.

'I could have told you that,' Margaret retorted. 'Jennie has a terrific capacity for affection but it was getting blocked off in all the wrong channels. Miles was wrong for her. She didn't need a plaster saint, she needed a man. Wait and discover how nice she is, John.'

'Of course she's nice. Once I saw her in that ridiculous club of hers, I knew why she acted the way she did. David is going to make her a happy woman. Thank heaven, he has finally forgiven me for keeping him away from her. But I didn't want Beatrice to know Jennie was in the clear.'

'All Jennie needed was the assurance that she was loved. In a way,' Margaret added, 'that's all any woman needs.'

'And speaking of that,' Harland began.

He was interrupted as the door opened and David and Jennie came in. Harland glanced from one radiant face to the other. 'While you are working for me,' he said severely, 'I shall expect you to be punctual.'

'I'm sorry, sir,' David said, 'but I'm looking for a permanent job now. I'm going to support a wife.'

'The job with me is permanent if you want it.'

'Do you mean that?' David asked eagerly.

Harland nodded. 'Man is still his own worst enemy and he'll go on plunging himself into trouble and crime. For a long time to come there will be plenty of work.' He looked at the young couple and smiled. 'But for the present,' he added, 'there is ample time for a honeymoon.'

'Come on,' David said, reaching for Jennie's hand, 'let's get out of here. We've got things to decide.'

When they had gone Harland turned to Margaret. 'As I was saying,' he began firmly.